'The Flower Girls

Violet and Rose, uprooted and entwined by war

PENNY WILSON

THE CHOIR PRESS

First published in the United Kingdom in 2024 by
The Choir Press

ISBN 978-1-78963-468-6

For my mother, who believed in me
For Andrew, who supported me
Never forgetting Jemima

Contents

Prologue – 1942

$\mathcal{R}$ose ran up the stairs, stumbling at the top in her haste. The carpet was even more threadbare than she remembered. Nothing in England had changed, but after the bright modern house in New York everything looked tired and dingy. Wealth in England was not ostentatious, she remembered, it was old and ancestral.

No one had come to meet her off the boat at Southampton. Father had sent a car with his chauffeur, not Briggs, he must have signed up to fight, but an older man who had driven in silence all the way to Chalworth, only remarking to Mrs Sproat when they arrived, 'Bloomin' waste of petrol.'

Mrs Sproat had answered the door. American maids wore uniforms. Mrs S had a dirty apron on. She looked worn and her swollen feet were stuffed into once fluffy slippers.

'Your mother's got one of her heads,' was all she said. Then added, 'She got the telegram but didn't know when you'd get here.'

Rose had not missed her mother or Mrs Sproat, or any of them. All she wanted to do was get her jodhpurs on and see Mousie.

The door to Rose's old bedroom was open. It was a sunny July afternoon, but the curtains were drawn across the window to stop the sun's rays damaging the furniture. Her single bed looked small after the large brass-framed double she had slept in at Number 48. It was covered in the familiar white eider-down strewn with pink roses. The bookshelves were dusty. Someone had arranged the books in order of height. A collection of china dolls Father had brought back for her from his diplomatic travels looked ghoulish in the gloomy light of the room. Two of them had plaits in their hair. Rose had always brushed the hair straight, leaving it flowing over their shoulders.

A chest of drawers next to the washstand under the window had a drawer half sticking out as if someone had tried and failed to close it in a hurry. Rose saw her face reflected back at her from the dressing-table mirror above the drawers. She looked hot and sweaty; the sea air had played havoc with her already frizzy hair, and her eyes had shrunk into her puffy face. *I look like a pig*, she thought, wondering if she would fit into her jodhpurs now. She had eaten well at the Wisemans'; rationing had not hit the wealthy suburbs of New York, even after the Americans had entered the war. Rose had breasts, hips and a well-rounded stomach. None of the clothes she had gone to America with fitted her anymore.

Rose rummaged through the half-open drawer. There was no sign of her jodhpurs or her riding shirt. She went out onto the landing.

'Mrs Sproat! Where are my riding things?' she shouted.

No reply. Her mother's bedroom door remained firmly closed. There had been mention in one of her mother's infre-quent letters of a new maid. It must be her day off. Rose felt a strong urge to stamp her foot and scream. As a child it had been effective, but today it seemed only the grandfather clock was listening. Its rhythmic tick would ignore her demand.

'To hell with it!' said Rose out loud. A useful phrase she had picked up from Mr Wiseman. Rose shuddered at the thought of him. Mother would not approve of her new vocabulary, but it felt just right to say it now. She would go down the lane to the farm in her travelling clothes to see Mousie, picking up some carrots on the way. Nothing else mattered.

There were no carrots in the larder and no sign of her riding boots by the back door. She could see Mrs S in her snug off the kitchen, slumped with her feet up listening to the radio. Rose let herself out and stomped down the road towards the farm –

some homecoming. If her shoes got ruined, Mrs S could jolly well clean them.

For all its supposed cleanliness, comfort and general affability, nothing in America came close to the bucolic charm of Froggetts Farm. The low farmhouse with its tiled roof and lead-paned windows was so much a part of the landscape it might as well have grown up out of the soil, with shoots of outbuildings sprouting on one side and fields stretching away into the distance on the other. Some of the fields had horses in, but Rose could not make out Mousie in any of them. It was a warm day; maybe Mr Turner had put him in a stable to keep cool. She could see the farmer down by the stream fixing some fencing.

Behind the house was a wood with a narrow track that led from the wood to the yard. The log that Mr Turner's son, George, had put alongside the track for Rose when she was learning to jump was still there. How impatient she was to ride again.

There was a distant sound of horses' hooves coming closer, then a high-pitched shriek. Out of the wood came Mousie at full pelt, with a slim hatless girl balanced on top, urging him on and laughing.

'Too slow!' shouted the girl, turning her head to watch as a young man on a sturdy cob emerged from the trees. 'Come on, Mousie. We can do it.' The girl pointed Mousie at the jump. 'Hup!' she said as they cleared the log easily, landing safely on the other side.

It was a scene straight out of the movies Rose had watched at the New York Picture House. This was the moment the handsome hero rode alongside the wild gypsy girl, swung her out of the saddle and onto his horse before kissing her passionately as the credits rolled.

The young man, she realised with a start, was George. He had been a boy when Rose left. She had never paid him much attention other than getting him to move jumps for her. American boys had scared Rose. They had a brittle layer of polish on them, as did the girls. There was no polish on this man. Both he and the girl looked as naturally beautiful as their surroundings. George was holding his hands up in mock surrender and bowing to the triumphant girl.

'I swear you put magic in that pony, Vi.'

'Yeah! The only magic is not having to carry a great lump like you around.'

George opened his mouth to protest. Then stopped. He saw Rose standing at the end of the track. George slowly lowered his arms.

'Get off,' he hissed at the girl. She stuck her tongue out at him.

'Poor loser.'

'No, just get off now.'

George leant down and took hold of Mousie's bridle. The girl looked across to where Rose stood. Her face, so full of laughter, darkened into a sullen stare. She slid off the side of the little pony. The girl looked taller on the ground. Her jodhpurs were Rose's. They fitted her neatly, but her long legs meant there was a gap at the bottom between them and Rose's brown jodhpur boots.

'You'd best go,' said George, holding on to the pony.

The girl started down the track towards Rose. She twirled her riding crop nonchalantly in one hand, taking in Rose's brown pleated skirt – tight around her waist – the yellow aertex shirt and the sensible lace-up shoes. As she drew alongside Rose, she stopped and dropped the riding crop.

'You'll be too big for him now,' said the girl, before continuing slowly down the track to the yard. 'You'll see,' she shouted back at Rose as she disappeared behind the big barn.

Throughout the three-week crossing from America, with the all-pervasive fear of German torpedoes, intermittent bouts of seasickness and an overwhelming sense of wretchedness, Rose had been sustained by thoughts of her pony and how pleased he would be to see her. Yet here he was having fun in the hands of another.

George had dismounted from the cob and was leading both horses towards her.

'You're back then.'

Rose nodded. She wanted to cry. George handed her Mousie's reins.

'Vi's been exercising him for you,' he muttered.

Mousie's head was down. He was sweating and breathing heavily.

'How dare she ride him like that!'

It all started to unravel, the powerlessness Rose had felt at the grasping hands of Mr Wiseman, the long journey, and now this final crushing of expectation. Rose picked up the riding crop Vi had left on the ground. She started screaming and hitting out at George with the whip.

'He's mine. You had no right. Who is she?'

'Whoa there, girl.' Mr Turner was approaching them across the field. 'Put that down,' he said firmly to Rose. 'You're scaring the horses. Control yourself.' Rose lowered the riding crop, sobbing loudly. She had always been a bit scared of Mr Turner. He had taught her to ride and was the only person who ever stood up to her. 'Take the horses back to the yard and wash them down,' he said quietly to George. 'And you, go home, miss. Come back tomorrow when you can behave like a lady.'

CHAPTER 1

Violet – September 1939

*T*he sudden jolt woke Vi. It had happened before, the feeling of falling down a step just as she was going off to sleep. Now she would lie awake staring at the ceiling she could not see in the darkness. Absorbing the cold. If only she could keep falling and not wake; the empty nothingness of sleep beyond the step.

Vi stretched out her arm along the hard, lumpy mattress. Her mother was not there. She was usually late back on a Saturday night. The single rug was hers, and Vi wrapped it around her. If her mother came back at all, there would be the stink of gin and shadowy bruises on her arms, sometimes her eyes. Vi does not dare move if there are bruises. Her mother groans in her sleep if there are bruises.

Tomorrow is Sunday. The thought is a comfort to Vi as she curls up under the blanket and waits for sleep to come again.

Her mother was not back in the morning. Vi reached under the bed, a grim grey light filtering through the grimy window of the room they both shared. She found the dress Mrs Horse had given her last month, navy with a white collar and cuffs. Her name wasn't really Horse, but Vi didn't know their names; she just saw their faces and smelt their fragrant perfumes and colognes. Sunday was church, and church was love and warmth.

Not the love of God. Vi didn't believe in God. If he was what all the people in the church said he was, then her life could not exist. But it did. She had discovered the church by accident on her way to the West End with Billy Bob to find rich pickings in the park. It had been a bleak January day and Vi was cold and tired. They had passed a church with a spire and a bell ringing out. The door had been open. Vi had ducked inside to escape the wind. She slunk down into one of the pews at the back, glad to be out of the wind and away from Billy Bob's entreaties of, 'Come on, Vi, keep up.'

It took a while before Vi could concentrate on what the minister was saying. Cold did that to Vi, limiting her ability to engage with the outside world. There was singing, then prayers.

'We pray for those less fortunate than ourselves; the cold, the weak, the hungry.'

'Amen,' said the congregation.

That's me, thought Vi, soaking up the prayers that were for her.

When Vi was little, her mother had sung to her and stroked her hair. But when her mother lost the job at Mr Ashton's haberdashery, the singing stopped. She came home late, if at all, and the bruises began.

The church was full of singing, of a better world, a marching to redemption. But more importantly it was full of wickedness. All the glorious ladies and gentlemen in that church believed they were wicked.

'We do not presume to come to this thy table on merciful lord, trusting in our own wickedness…'

That had been two years ago. Now Vi was eleven, and the little church with the big open door had taught her everything. People wanted to be good. Vi knew she was no longer good; stealing, lying, missing school, these were all bad things, but the key was humility.

'We humbly beseech thee, O Lord.'

'Lead us not into temptation, but deliver us from evil.'

The congregation repeated the same words every week. They were looking for salvation. *I can be their salvation*, Vi realised. All she had to do was stand at the back of the church looking humble as the ladies and gentlemen filed out.

'Oh my! Poor little mite.'

'Give her something, James. Look, her boots are hardly held together.'

Vi kept her eyes down, her hands by her side. A small whiskered gentleman leant towards her and pressed a coin into her hand.

'Here, take this,' he said, moving away as quickly as possible, his wife patting him on the arm as they left the church together, their heads held high.

They got quite used to seeing Vi at the back of the church and would bring her cast-off clothes and boots.

'Where are your parents?' they would ask.

'Mother is sick,' Vi would mutter. 'I pray for her.'

After the service, Vi ran down the narrow alleyway alongside the church where Billy Bob was waiting.

'A good haul today,' said Vi, opening a brown package one of the ladies had handed her.

'For your mother,' the woman had said.

There was a triangular slice of pork pie and a hunk of fruitcake. Vi divided both carefully. Then she set upon each portion with relish.

'The Germans are coming,' said Vi. 'The vicar said so. They were not praying for the poor today, they were praying for themselves and their families.'

Billy Bob was wearing his usual top hat, a moleskin waistcoat over a collarless shirt and a tutu. It was fun to dress him in a different way to everybody else. Nobody but her could see him, so it did not matter. Vi had got the idea for a tutu from a poster she had seen alongside one of the theatres in the West End. The picture showed a line of the most beautiful girls Vi had ever seen standing on their toes in a line, linking arms. All the girls were looking down at her in a way that made Vi feel cross. Vi found a small tear and she ripped the poster up the centre from the bottom. When it was too high for her to reach, she yanked the paper hard and the tear went all the way to the top. The line of girls collapsed awkwardly off the wall.

That had been a few days ago. Since then, Billy Bob had worn the tutu every day, much to his disgust and Vi's delight.

It was a warm September day as Vi and Billy Bob walked slowly back towards the East End of London. There were churches there, but had she stood at the back looking sad, she would have got a clip round the ear. Vi was not in a hurry to get home. She wandered along the river enjoying the cool breeze that came off the murky water. It seemed everyone she passed was talking about war and the Germans coming. People were not sauntering in their usual manner. They were purposeful and engaged in deep conversation.

Vi remembered seeing Germany on the big world map at the school she had gone to when her mother had a job. In those days, Vi had gone to school every day with pigtails in her hair, a clean handkerchief in her pocket and boots without holes. Billy Bob was not there then. Vi had other friends: Muriel and Winifred. They had played hopscotch together and vied to outdo each other in their reading and writing. When Vi's mother started drinking the gin and coming home late at night, Vi's friends did not want to play with her anymore.

'Something stinks,' Muriel would say, turning away from Vi. 'Can you smell it, Winnie?'

'Disgusting!' Winnie agreed, holding her nose. 'Come on! I can't breathe.'

When Vi cried, they called her a cry-baby. It was Billy Bob who had come to her rescue. He appeared beside her one morning as she went through the school gates. He was dressed then like all the other boys, in short trousers, braces and a flannel shirt. She had not seen him at school before. She generally avoided boys; they were rough and called the girls rude names. His name, he said, was 'Billy Bob. My ma wanted to call me Billy and my dad wanted Bob.' *How nice to have a mother and father who worked like that*, was all Vi could think. She had never had a dad.

'Stick your foot out as they both go by, you'll get one of

them,' Billy Bob said. Vi looked round nervously. The other children did not like her much anymore, and suggestions like that were going to make things worse. No one was taking any notice. Billy Bob was smiling at her encouragingly. 'Go on.' His face was round and cheerful, like the gingerbread men she had made with her mother. A currant nose and two currant eyes; they had never given them a mouth. Billy Bob had a mouth full of bright white teeth. His hair was not ginger; it was the colour of the straw Mr Atkins, the rag-and-bone man, put in the stable for his horse, Fred.

That morning, Winifred swung through the gates arm in arm with Muriel. Vi stuck her foot out, catching Muriel's ankle and sending her flying, half pulling Winifred down with her.

'Nice work,' said Billy Bob.

School had faded out of Vi's life after that. She could read and write reasonably well. Keeping warm, finding food and roaming the streets with Billy Bob were more important to her now. Vi's mother did not seem to notice, which made it all the more remarkable when Vi arrived home after all the talk she had heard of war and her mother was waiting for her, looking more normal than usual and also talking of war.

'You've got to go, Vi,' she said. 'The Germans are coming. All the children are going to the countryside. They are going to kill us in our beds and burn our houses down. You've got to go, girl.'

Everyone called Vi's mother Bonnie – her real name was Elsie. She had been bonny once and still dressed up well to go out at night, but during the day she rarely got out of her night-dress. Today, she had made an effort: there were clips in her hair, shoes on her feet and she was wearing a relatively clean pale blue dress covered in yellow flowers. Vi wanted to give her a hug, but her mother did not like hugs anymore. She was pacing up and down, waving a piece of paper at Vi and becoming increasingly distraught.

'Just go!' said her mother, throwing the piece of paper at Vi before reaching for the bottle of gin on the table.

Vi went out onto the street with the paper. Billy Bob was waiting. He never went inside. The two of them slipped through a gap in Mr Atkins' fence. It was Sunday; he would not be working today. Vi read the typed words slowly.

'It says all the children have got to go to school tomorrow with their suitcase, then they will get on a train and go to live in the countryside without their parents until it is safe.'

Vi tried to imagine the countryside. She had seen pictures in the books at school. There had been a cow in a field with a story about milk. All the pictures had been green and clean, with the sun shining: a far cry from the grey grime of the East End of London and all the fears that came at night when her mother did not come home.

'Shall we go, Billy Bob?' Vi looked at him. He had taken the tutu off and was wearing men's trousers held up with string. He looked older.

'We'd be running away,' he said. 'But then I suppose we are always running away. You don't get caught if you run away.'

CHAPTER 2

Rose – September 1939

*T*he notion that she was spoilt had never occurred to Rose. Growing up in a household where quiet was constantly in demand, Rose had learnt that noise got her exactly what she wanted.

Lady Symes, Rose's mother, suffered – everyone said – from nervous exhaustion. Sir Reginald, her father, took himself off to London at every opportunity, leaving his Surrey home, his fragile wife and his noisy daughter to get on with life without him. Today, however, he was in the drawing room telling Rose she was to go and live in America.

'There's a war coming. The German will invade. It is not safe for you here. The Wisemans have said they will have you. The ship leaves in two days.'

The words were delivered in short, sharp bursts like the volley of shots that rang out when the shoot annihilated the pheasants in the cover crop.

Lady Symes was lying on the elegant chaise longue in the bay window, looking out onto the love-knot garden Sir Reginald Symes had designed for his young wife in the early days of their marriage. At the mention of war, she gave a low moan and raised her hand to her eyes as if shielding her person, in the only way she knew, from a German onslaught.

Sir Reginald had served in the 4th/7th Hussars before joining the Foreign Office. In his world, orders were given and received down the chain of command without fuss or explanation. He rang the bell for Mrs Sproat, the housekeeper. Her prompt appearance led Rose to think she must have been listening at the door. Mrs Sproat's swollen ankles were normally her excuse for a delayed entrance.

'I want you to pack Miss Rose's things, take one of the cases, and have her ready to leave at eight o'clock tomorrow morning. She'll need warm clothes for the journey and some school-books to keep her occupied. Do you understand?'

'Oh my!' said Mrs Sproat. She wanted to add 'poor little mite', but there was nothing poor, little or mitish about Rose. As for schoolbooks, there had not been a governess for at least a year; none of them would put up with the child. 'Yes, sir.' It would be a relief to get rid of the girl, with all her temper tantrums. Good luck, America. The Germans were not coming to England, Mr Chamberlain had said so on the radio; she could put her feet up with only Lady S to look after.

Rose had not moved since she had entered the room. Her father had asked to see her immediately when he had arrived unexpectedly from London that morning. Here she was stand-ing underneath the austere couple of Victorian ancestors mounted in gold frames perpetually judging her, with events suddenly moving along beyond her control. She was tall for eleven, closely resembling her father, with his broad shoulders and strong features. The only bit of her that she shared with her mother was a small pouting mouth.

'I'm not going. I won't go. I don't care about the Germans.' Rose started to cry. Her voice was not working well. She did not feel strong in front of the imposing presence of her father. He stood in front of the marble fireplace, his legs apart, hands behind his back, eyes front, ignoring his daughter's pleas.

'Briggs will drive us to London in the morning, and I will see you onto the Liverpool train. Mrs Sproat, you will look after my wife. I shall be in London for the foreseeable future.'

With that, Sir Reginald strode from the room. 'I will be in my study. I don't want to be disturbed.'

Not only did Rose always get what she wanted, she never did what she did not want. But there was no appealing to her mother. Lady Symes was emitting soft mewling sounds like a kitten and gesturing for her smelling salts. Mrs Sproat was fussing about her mistress, ignoring Rose and looking decidedly pleased with the way things were turning out.

Rose stamped her foot in frustration.

'I'm going to run away with Mousie. You'll never find me. The Germans won't find me. You'll be sorry. I hate you.'

Mousie was Rose's pony. He lived down the lane on Mr Turner's farm. The previous Christmas, Aunt Maud – her father's older sister – had given Rose a book, *Moorland Mousie*. Once she had read it, all Rose wanted was a Mousie of her own. Fortunately, Aunt Maud, of whom she was not particularly fond given the similarities to her brother, had announced that all girls should learn to ride. 'It's excellent for the constitution, and the gel will bag herself a decent husband on the hunting field once the time comes.' Aunt Maud had a low opinion of Rose's mother and felt it her duty to keep her niece on the right track.

For her eleventh birthday, Aunt Maud gave Rose Mousie. He was really called Basil and had belonged to Aunt Maud's youngest daughter, but from the moment he arrived he was Rose's Mousie.

It was a Sunday morning. Mr Turner gave her a riding lesson on Sundays in return for her mucking out the horses while he was at church. Rose had been heading to the farm when her father summoned her. She ran there now, not bothering to put on her jodhpurs or her boots, tears of frustration streaking her face.

The farm was quiet. Mr Turner would still be at church with his son, George. Mousie was grazing in the field with the two other horses that lived on the yard.

Rose climbed over the wooden gate and flung herself against his warm, solid neck.

'I'll never leave you. They can't make me. I am going to take you away. We'll hide in the woods and you can eat the grass and drink from the stream. I can live off acorns and blackberries.'

Mousie looked up expectantly. Rose usually arrived with carrots. He flicked the flies from his eyes with his silver-grey forelock. There was no sign of any carrots. He went back to eating the grass.

A voice rang out across the field. 'You're a bit late this morning, miss. Those stables need doing. I've got some nice cavaletti poles for you to jump later. George made them up. I haven't got long.'

Mr Turner was a busy man and always had better things to do than teach Rose. She had been a right madam at the beginning, not listening to anything he said, never accepting criticism. The pony was a good one, but even he had got fed up when the girl kept bashing her heels into his ribs and had given a sudden violent buck one day, throwing Rose out of the saddle and into a muddy puddle. After that, Rose began to listen and was turning into a good little rider.

'Go and see what's up, George. I'm going in to change out of my church clothes.'

George was a year older than Rose. He was long and gangly like a young colt and vaulted the gate with ease. He stood looking across the field at Rose, who was lying on the grass beside her pony, sobbing. People, George believed, were no different from animals. Look after them well and they thrived. In Rose he saw a creature that was uncared for, who screamed and yelled because no one fed and watered her soul. He could never have articulated these thoughts; they were simply part of his understanding of the world.

'It may never happen,' he said, moving alongside her. 'Do you want a hand up?'

Rose took his hand and let him pull her up off the grass.

'It has. It already has,' she said. Rose no more knew how to run away than she knew how to fly to the moon.

CHAPTER 3

Violet – A Bus, a Train and Cartwheels

Vi leapt onto the old school bus as the driver attempted to close the door. The handle needed replacing. It was always a bit of an effort to make sure the old girl shut properly.

'Oi! Look out!'

The bus driver shouted as Vi pushed past him. The canvas bag Vi was carrying got tangled around her legs and she fell, sprawling, into the aisle of the bus. There was laughter and shouting from the children in the neat rows of seats.

'Look what the cat dragged in.'

'Stowaway!'

'Who's going to want her?'

'Not the Germans.'

'Oh, it's you,' said Mrs Mundy. 'You're not on my list.'

Mrs Mundy ran the school that Vi had attended in happier times. She had thought Vi showed promise until she started absconding and lashing out at other pupils.

The bus lurched forward. Vi attempted to stand up but only managed to slump into the empty front seat next to Mrs Mundy. She could see Billy Bob's feet dangling down in the windscreen of the bus. He must be sitting on the roof.

'I'm evacuating,' said Vi, waving a piece of paper at Mrs Mundy. 'I've got my bag and my name and a coat.' The note had said to wear warm clothes and pack a bag. Vi did not have a bag, but she had found an old potato sack at the back of Mr Atkins' yard. It smelt mouldy, like mushrooms with bits of soil embedded in the hessian. Packing had not taken long. Vi had a dress and a jumper from the church ladies. She was wearing a skirt and cardigan that were both too small for her and a coat that was far too big. It was her mother's. Vi had taken it from the hook on the back of the door while her mother slept. The coat was red with a small stand-up collar, nipped-in waist and full skirt. Vi was very hot.

Mrs Mundy had a clipboard with a long list of names stuck to it. She added Vi's name. It had been a long morning. All those tears as parents handed over their children. In her experience, parents were generally happy to get rid of their offspring. Once she had seen this lot onto the train, Mrs Mundy was off to stay with her sister in Hastings. If there was a war coming, families had to stick together.

The children were quiet as the bus drew up outside Waterloo Station. Its grand stone entrance was a gapping mouth that would swallow them up and disgorge them into another world.

Mrs Mundy lined them up in crocodile formation. Winifred and Muriel were holding hands near the front. Muriel was crying. Winifred squeezed her hand.

'Cheer up, Muriel. Mam says there's chickens and cream in the country. We'll get to live on a farm with all the food you want.'

They glared at Vi as she walked past. Vi stopped and stepped forward towards her two ex-friends.

'There's spiders and snakes and rats the size of dogs. They feed little girls to them to keep them happy. That's why they want us in the countryside,' she told them in a conspiratorial whisper.

Muriel screamed. Johnny Brown and his little brother, Sam, were delighted. Muriel was always telling them off and getting them into trouble.

'Yeah! They fatten you up with all that cream then they feed you to the pigs,' said Johnny. 'Only boys are safe, because they can be useful and help with the feeding.'

The station concourse was a seething mass of children and

wailing parents. Billy Bob joined Vi at the back of the line.

'Come on. We need to get away from this lot. Where do you fancy, Vi?'

There was a group of ladies making their way through the throng of children. They reminded Vi of her church ladies, with their hats and feathers and lingering smell of lilies.

'We're following them,' she said. 'We're going to G U I L D F O R D.' She spelt out the name above the platform. A train was waiting and the ladies were getting on it. Billy Bob took off his top hat with a flourish, bowed low to Vi then did a series of cartwheels along the platform.

'We're going to Guildford. We're going to Guildford,' he called out as he whirled and twirled and weaved his way through the heaving mass of fleeing Londoners.

The train carriage Vi stepped into had a long passageway down one side, with a line of individual compartments on the other. She paused to absorb the stillness after the chaos of the platform. The doors to each of the compartments had glass windows with a sign underneath that read, 'RESERVED St Martha's School'. Vi peered into the first one. There were two rows of girls facing each other, with the racks above their heads neatly filled with small suitcases. They reminded Vi of the display of dolls she had seen lined up in a window of a toyshop in London. All the girls wore identical navy blue coats buttoned to the top, with matching navy hats adorned with a plain maroon ribbon around the crown. The next compartment was filled with the same identical group, and the next and the one after that.

A shout went up. 'All aboard!' Doors slammed, a whistle blew and the train lumbered forward. Vi was thrown against one of the compartment doors. It clicked open. Vi steadied herself on the doorframe. Ten pairs of eyes looked up expectantly at her, one pair from over the top of tortoiseshell glasses now slightly askew from the movement of the train. The owner of the glasses was the only grown-up in the compartment.

'Who are you? What are you doing?' said the grown-up, adjusting her glasses and staring fiercely at Vi.

It had been a long time since Vi had cried. Billy Bob had told her, 'Crying is weak. People take advantage when you're weak. You've gotta fight, Violet.' And so Vi had. But he was not by her side now. She felt totally alone and heading, with every quickening turn of the wheels, further away from all she knew.

'If I squeeze up, she can sit here, Miss Stretton.' A girl next to the woman was patting a small space beside her on the bench seat. 'You're going to fall over. You must sit down,' she said to Vi, smiling encouragingly at her. Holding back the tears, Vi sank gratefully into the space. These girls were neat and tidy, like the churchgoers. *This is a time for humble*, thought Vi.

'I am heartily sorry,' she murmured. 'I do not presume.' Vi kept her eyes down, clasped her hands together and tried to remember what the congregation repeated each week.

Vi had squeezed in next to Miss Stretton, the Deputy Head of St Martha's School for Girls. Her job was to keep order, ensure everything went smoothly and the girls behaved in a manner befitting young ladies. So far this morning she had done her job well; uprooting an entire school from London to a large house in the Surrey countryside was a challenge. Having got all the girls on the train, Miss Stretton was allowing herself a moment of self-congratulation. Phase one had gone without a hitch. Now this extraordinary creature had landed among them. A stick of a girl in an oversized red coat, no hat, straggly brown hair, a very flushed face and clutching what looked like a potato sack. The girl appeared to be reciting the Scriptures.

'These seats are reserved for St Martha's girls. You probably need to be somewhere else.' There was a slight musty smell coming off the girl. This matter needed to be sorted.

Vi started on the Lord's Prayer. 'Our Father who art in Heaven.' The occupants of the compartment were well-brought-up girls and knew never to interrupt prayers. Vi's voice tuned in to the rhythm of the train.

'... the power and the glory, for ever and ever,' then came to a sudden stop with a quiet 'Amen.'

'Amen,' said Miss Stretton, unable to stop this conditioned response in the midst of a difficult moment. Already, the approach of war was turning their lives upside down; perhaps this girl was a symbol of faith in a topsy-turvy world. Miss Stretton had a strong faith and believed in angels. This one was in an unlikely guise. The girl was attempting to remove her coat with Pamela's help. She was a kind girl, Pamela, but offering this girl a seat was really too much.

'I'll put this up here.' Pamela braced herself against the movement of the train and pushed Vi's coat on top of the suit-cases. 'I'm Pamela. What's your name?' she asked. 'Do you want me to take that too?' All the girls stared at Vi's potato sack.

With Billy Bob by her side, Vi had learnt that anger triumphed over fear, so when people sneered at her she lashed out. But these people were not sneering at her; they just seemed curious.

'No, it's fine here.' Vi hid the sack behind her legs. 'I got separated from my friend, Billy Bob. Then I got on this train and I'm going to Guildford. I'm evacuating from the Germans. Violet, my name is Violet.'

'We're going to Guildford,' said Pamela brightly. 'You can stay with us. I expect someone will meet you at the other end.'

Vi doubted anyone would, but she nodded. 'I expect so,' she said, leaning back into the narrow space.

One of the smaller girls on the bench across from Vi started to cry.

'I want to go home,' she sobbed. The girl next to her put an arm around the young girl's shoulders.

'Let's sing a song to cheer us all up,' said Miss Stretton. 'We must all be brave little soldiers. Come on, after me.

'Onward Christian soldiers marching as to war ...'

It was Vi's favourite hymn. She knew all the words and let them flow freely out of her mouth into the warmth and comfort of the cramped little railway carriage.

CHAPTER 4

Rose – And a Boat

There was no one for Rose to wave to from the deck of the *Sumaria* as she pulled slowly away from Liverpool Docks. Rose waved anyway. A band on the quayside was playing *Onward Christian Soldiers*, while the sun glinted off their instruments. After the long train journey from London and a cramped night on a camp bed in a crowded hotel, it was liberating to be standing on the deck of a ship with seagulls whirling around overhead. The strong sea breeze caught Rose's hat and carried it off over the churning waves. A cheer went up. Rose waved at her hat.

'Goodbye, hat. Goodbye, England.'

Rose had felt numb since hugging Mousie for the last time. She had wordlessly followed her father and done as he said. What she had not expected was this glorious sense of expectation, of being on an adventure.

'Britain,' said the sandy-haired boy standing next to her. 'Goodbye, Britain. We're from Scotland, not England. Typical English, you always assume we all are.'

'Don't mind him, lass. You watch your manners, young David.' A little bird-like woman, not much bigger than the boy, was standing alongside him, holding a smaller boy up against the railings. 'Are you on your own, dear?'

'Sorry, I didn't mean to be rude. I'm David.' The sandy-haired boy put out his hand for Rose to shake. She was not accustomed to shaking hands or being pleasant to others. Rose stared at the hand. 'Quite right. All a bit formal,' said David, lowering his arm. 'We're going to New York to stay with Uncle Arthur, just until the war is over. Pa says it won't take long. We have the best army in the world. I'm going to an American school. I don't expect they will play cricket, but Pa says I can teach them.'

The little boy, not wanting to be outdone by his big brother, tried to get Rose's attention.

'You can call me Aub. My real name is Aubrey but everyone calls me Aub. Can you play Snap? We have got cards in our cabin. Mrs Mac says we are going to play Snap all the way to New York.'

They were all smiling at Rose. She found herself smiling back.

'I don't know how to play Snap, perhaps you can teach me. My name's Rosemary, but you can call me Rose.' Aub looked delighted. Somehow, Rose had said just the right thing. Aub climbed down from the rail onto the deck and took Rose's hand in his. It was as soft and reassuring as Mousie's velvet nose.

So began three weeks of freedom and friendship. Mrs Mac took to her cabin on the first day with a bad case of seasickness. It was a worry; the boys' parents had entrusted her to look after their children, but David was a sensible child. They couldn't leave the ship and with that nice girl Rose helping, they could manage Aub between them. The ship became their playground, as it did for all their fellow travellers. It did not take David long to establish a cricket pitch on the top deck. He had a cricket bat in his luggage but had to make do with tennis balls after the first morning, when his opening batsman sent the one and only cricket ball out to sea.

Aub never left Rose's side.

'Come on, lazy bones, let's get breakfast.' Aub ran into her cabin every morning and bounced on the bed until she got up. He was an angelic-looking child. Everyone assumed Rose was his sister. They became a popular pair with the crew.

'Chef wants to meet the young man who is eating all his porridge,' said the purser to Rose one morning after breakfast. So they followed him down to the enormous galley kitchen. It was full of men in tall white hats stirring bubbling pots over huge hot stoves. The tallest and broadest of these men came over to Rose and Aub.

'We want some cake,' demanded Aub.

'Say please,' Rose added.

'Please can we have some cake?'

The chef was a bear of a man. He scooped Aub off the ground easily and held him up for inspection.

'Where are you going to put it?' he asked.

'In my tummy,' said Aub, lifting up his shirt.

A trip to the kitchen became a daily routine for the two of them. Then they were invited up to the bridge, where the ship's captain let Aub wear his hat and have a go at steering the ship.

'Why are there all those other big ships?' Aub demanded. 'Are they all going to America too?'

Rose and the captain exchanged looks. Rose knew David's theory on the accompanying warship and frigates.

'Protection,' David had told her knowledgeably. 'Not just for us. Wouldn't surprise me if we had treasure on board going to safety too. Crown jewels, I expect. Mind you, they can't do much against a German submarine.' Rose had not taken him seriously, but standing up on the bridge, it did seem like a cordon of ships was gathered around them.

'Why are they all painted yellow?' said Aub, pointing at the warship steaming alongside them.

'I expect it's to cheer us all up,' Rose told him. He didn't need to know David's complicated theory, which she had not really understood, all about submarine periscopes and yellow being a good camouflage colour.

The chief engineer took them into the engine room to see all the pumping pistons. It was a smelly place and they both felt a bit sick. Back on deck, the fresh air restored them. Aub skipped and hopped and charmed all the mummies and nannies watching from long reclining chairs. For the first time in Rose's life, she was popular. She basked in little Aub's good nature.

'What are you going to do when we get to New York?' Aub asked Rose one evening, after their umpteenth game of Snap. 'Mrs Mac says we'll be there soon.'

David was sitting next to them reading his New York guide-book. He looked up, waiting for Rose's answer. He had got used to having Rose around and had forgotten she was not part of their long-term plan.

Rose was enjoying her life in limbo. She did not want to think about any sort of future, but both boys were looking at her expectantly. An old familiar sulk settled on Rose's face.

'I'm going to stay with some people called Wiseman. Father knows Mr Wiseman through collecting stamps.'

'Stamps!' said David. 'Like I have in my stamp book?'

'A bit bigger than that. Grown-ups collect them and sell them around the world for a lot of money. Father has done it for years and Mr Wiseman too. They have never met, but Mr Wiseman said they had a big house and could look after me during the war. I don't really know why.'

'Not your uncle then?' Aub looked confused. 'We've never met Uncle Arthur, but he's going to be just like Pa, only older. Mrs Mac says he's very funny.'

'I'm sure you will be fine,' said David. Anyone who collects stamps has got to be nice. If they have got a big house, they'll have lots of servants. We can come and see you.' David was nodding encouragingly at Rose.

Rose walked up onto the deck. The sun was setting across the endless ocean. Only it was not endless. Rose had never felt so alone.

A few days later, the New York skyline appeared on the horizon. It was far more impressive than that of Liverpool.

'Those are called skyscrapers. That's the Statue of Liberty.' David kept up a running commentary as the ship drew nearer and nearer to its destination.

Mrs Mac had helped Rose to pack her things.

'Here's our address, dear,' she said, slipping a card into Rose's bag. 'If you need us, you can come and find us.' Rose hugged her. There was not much to hug, but Rose did not want to let her go.

CHAPTER 5

Violet – The Countryside

It had been a trying morning for Mrs Sproat. Lady Symes, who had never shown the slightest interest in her daughter, had gone into a decline at the loss of her now beloved child.

'The poor darling going to the other side of the world without me; she may be sunk by Germans. I will never see my baby girl again.'

The doctor had left some sleeping draughts for Lady Symes. Mrs Sproat gave her mistress one, hoping for a bit of peace and quiet for herself. But now there was a loud knocking at the front door.

'Good morning, Mrs Sproat. Is Lady Symes at home?'

In the doorway stood Mrs Fortescue, who to all intents and purposes ran the village of Chalworth. She was a vision of efficiency in tweed.

'We are asking everyone in the village to take in an evacuee – or two,' she added hopefully. 'The children of London are in great danger. Our duty is to offer them our homes and our hearts in their hour of need.'

'Lady Symes is indisposed, but I am quite sure she will not want some grubby little London brat in the house.'

Mrs Fortescue looked the housekeeper up and down, taking in her swollen ankles, breathlessness and general sense of disarray.

'Some of the girls are quite old enough to take on work, go into service. Perhaps one of those …'

She let her words tail off for a moment, watching them sink in.

'They will be in the village hall at 3pm this afternoon. Good day to you.'

The hall in Chalworth was at the heart of the small village, hosting harvest festival suppers, parish meetings and the annual flower show. Vi found herself there in the same way empty paper bags got caught in a corner after tossing and turning on a breeze. The train from London had arrived at Guildford Station to much shouting and waving. The St Martha's girls had been lined up and marched away, leaving Vi standing on the platform. There was a train waiting on the other side of the platform. A guard waving a flag had ushered Vi onto it.

'Come along, we're about to depart.'

That had been it. After ten minutes, the train pulled up at the little station of Chalworth, and Vi was marshalled along a quiet road and into the village hall along with twenty or so tired, fractious children.

The nametag Vi had attached to a piece of string and tied around her neck had fallen off. No one had any record of her on their clipboards.

'You must be with someone.' A flustered lady in a tight straw hat was glaring at Vi.

No sign of Billy Bob; he must be waiting outside. She had not seen him since London. Vi put her hands together and closed her eyes as if in prayer.

'Lamb of God, that takest away the sins of the world, have mercy upon us.'

Humility and animals were worth a try in the country.

Mrs Sproat came into the hall and almost walked straight out again. There were children crying, their noses running; some even looked like they had soiled their trousers. The smell was extremely unpleasant; sick, urine and something she did not recognise – London probably. Standing against the far wall was a tall thin-faced girl, hands clasped in prayer. She almost looked grown up in her oversized coat. A God-fearing strong lass was exactly what Mrs Sproat needed in her life right now.

'I'll have that one!' shouted Mrs Sproat, pointing at Vi and elbowing her way through the crowd.

The clipboard lady was only too happy to rid herself of the problem Vi presented. She poked Vi's arm with her pencil.

'Yes. That's fine. What's your name? I'll make a note that you are going up to The Manor. How old are you?'

'Violet Mary Green. I'm eleven,' mumbled Vi. She did not like the look of the red-faced woman who had claimed her as if she were something to be picked up in a shop. The other children were being looked over in the same way; some by kindly couples, others by sour-faced single ladies with lace handkerchiefs held to their noses.

'You won't be needing school then,' said the clipboard lady.

It occurred to Violet that she had not actually thought about what she might do in the countryside. Singing with the St Martha's girls had been good, but they were probably much like all the other girls once they were in a school.

'I can read and write.' Vi looked up defiantly. Mrs Sproat hoped she was not going to be trouble.

'Right, Violet Green, you're coming with me. Pick up your things. There's a bit of a walk, and I haven't got time to stand about. You've taken up enough of my day already.'

Holt Manor was some way out of the village and although Vi's potato sack was not heavy, it began to weigh her down as she trailed along behind Mrs Sproat's large rhythmically swaying bottom.

Mrs Sproat kept up a stream of instructions at the beginning of the walk.

'Her Ladyship is not well, so she's not to be disturbed. You can have the room in the attic. You'll need to be up early in the morning to get the fires done, and there's the milk to be collected. This is not charity, you know.'

Vi spotted Billy Bob hanging from a tree at the side of the road. His legs were hooked over a low branch. He gave Vi an upside-down grin and sucked on a long piece of grass hanging out of his mouth.

'Bit of a tartar,' he said, putting his hands up to his ears and waggling them at Mrs Sproat. 'Nice round here, though. Bit more space and no Germans.' Billy Bob flipped his legs over the branch and landed alongside Vi.

'Is that your country look?' asked Vi, taking in his rough wool jacket, dark green tie and checked shirt. 'You look smart.'

'What did you say?' Mrs Sproat turned sharply to look at Vi. 'I'll not have you muttering your prayers. I am a God-fearing woman, but there's a time and a place. You can do church on Sundays once the chores are done.'

Billy Bob took Vi's hand and squeezed it.

'Yes, missus,' said Vi.

'Mrs Sproat to you. Now here we are. We might as well go through the front, no one will notice. You can take your things up to the attic then come and help me peel the potatoes for supper.'

Big stone gateposts marked the start of a long gravel drive leading to an imposing red-bricked house. It looked higgledy-piggledy to Vi. Windows jutted out at odd angles. The grand houses in London were balanced, with windows matching on either side of large front doors. This house did not match at all. It was ugly and ill fitting. The inside was no better. Wood-panelled walls dominated the entrance hall and main staircase before giving way to peeling grey paint at the top of the house and a small box room.

'This is for you. It's not been swept in a while. You can get a broom up here and tidy a bit. I can't keep coming up and down these stairs. You can fetch your water as well. There's a jug there.' Mrs Sproat pointed towards a low brown cupboard in the corner of the tiny room. 'You'll be needing a bath first.' The girl did not look too dirty, but it was not worth taking any chances. She was bound to have lice.

'Then you can put on some of Miss Rose's clothes. She's gone to America, you know. Doesn't matter if the Germans get the likes of you and me, but that little madam has to be kept safe.'

Safe? Vi had not felt safe for years. Was she safe now? Why had a girl been sent to America only for Vi to take her place? Vi sat down on the dark green and red tartan rug that covered the narrow bed – the only other furniture in the room. It looked soft and inviting. A bit of light was filtering through the dusty pane of a small dormer window. Vi could just make out a conker hanging from a piece of string in the centre of the glass. Billy Bob was watching over her.

'Though I walk through the shadow of the valley of death, I will fear no evil. Thy rod and thy …'

Words were coming out of the girl's mouth as she slowly curled herself up into a tight ball, wrapping the bright red coat around her. Her eyes closed. She was asleep.

Tenderness and poetry did not come naturally to Mrs Sproat.

'Look out for number one. No one else is going to,' was Mrs Sproat's motto, but the sight of this sliver of a thing on the bed tugged at something in her heart. Long-forgotten words came back to her.

> *Oh we'll lie quite still, not listen nor look,*
> *While the earth's bonds reel and shake,*
> *Lest, battered too long, our wall and we*
> *Should break … should break …*

Another war? Was it all going to happen again? Mrs Sproat had broken then. 'CORPORAL SPROAT LOST IN ACTION STOP', the telegram had read. Then her brother Ted, just one more eager young man among all those who never came back.

She closed the door on the sleeping child and went down-stairs for a cup of tea.

CHAPTER 6

Rose – New York

The Wisemans lived in a townhouse overlooking Central Park. They did not make their way to the docks to meet Rose off the boat, but sent their chauffeur, Maurice, in his smart brown uniform with shiny buttons and a neat peaked cap. He held aloft a large piece of white card with big black lettering. 'ROSE SYMES'.

Rose shrunk back behind Mrs Mac, who made her way towards the chauffeur, waving her arms to attract his attention.

'He's got black skin,' said Aub, pointing excitedly at Maurice.

Everyone on the dockside stopped what they were doing and looked up. Someone had screamed. It was Rose.

'Enough of that,' said Mrs Mac, putting her hand firmly on Rose's shoulder. 'Remember your manners! Thank you, young man,' she said, smiling at Maurice. 'This is Miss Rose. You can collect her trunk over there.' Mrs Mac pointed to the end of the vast ship where trunks and boxes were being unloaded onto trolleys.

'Don't go,' said Rose, hanging on to Mrs Mac's arm. 'I can't do this.'

Poor wee thing. Mrs Mac had grown fond of the child. All she had needed was a bit of love and responsibility, but now was not the time for sentimentality.

'Come along, boys, say your goodbyes. I can see your uncle over there. You keep in touch, Rose. It's the war, and we all have to do our bit. Now off you go.'

David put out his hand for her to shake. This time, she did. Aub hugged her tight.

'I love you, Rose.'

Then they were gone, rushing forward to greet a jolly-looking man in a voluminous driving coat. They did not turn back. Rose was alone with Maurice.

After weeks at sea, Rose felt light-headed and unsteady on her feet. She was grateful to sink into the deep leather of the car seat, trying not to brush against Maurice as he held the door open for her.

Everything was big in New York: the car, the chauffeur, the wide streets and the towering buildings. Posters on walls showed pretty smiling ladies in bright lipstick and grey-suited men holding cigarettes between gleaming white teeth.

They drove alongside a park stretching into the distance, and the car glided to a stop outside a grand set of steps. The door at the top opened simultaneously in a carefully choreographed movement, and there stood a neatly turned-out maid with skin as black as Maurice.

When Rose had started riding Mousie, Mr Turner's son, George, had persuaded her to jump on Mousie's back without a saddle when she collected the little pony from its field. Her first attempt had been scary; there was nothing to support her. Rose had panicked, screamed, frightened Mousie and fallen off. As she climbed the tall stone steps in New York, Rose felt completely unsupported, just as she had on her pony that day. She reached the open door and put her hand out to support herself on the doorframe before she fell. The maid grasped her hand and led her inside.

'This way, miss.'

Another door was opening; a cavernous drawing room lay beyond and Rose's unwanted, un-asked-for protectors.

Mr and Mrs Wiseman were both hugely fat. Mrs Sproat had been a bit large and baggy, but nothing like these two.

'Welcome, my dear,' said Mr Wiseman, in an American drawl that Rose had heard children on the boat trying to imitate. Mr Wiseman got up awkwardly from his chair and enveloped Rose in a hug. His overwhelming presence and sweet-smelling cologne would have knocked Rose off balance completely were it not for him holding her so tightly.

'Give the girl some air,' said Mrs Wiseman, not getting up but patting the space on the sofa beside her. 'Come and sit here. How was your journey? How are your parents? Have some candy.'

Mr Wiseman released his hold on her, and Rose staggered towards the sofa and the brightly coloured bowl of sweets Mrs Wiseman was holding out to her. Rose knew she would not make it. She was wobbly, her skin was clammy and her stomach was lurching uncontrollably; there was nothing to steady her. Rose fell forward and was sick all over Mrs Wiseman's capacious lap.

'Get it off! Get it off'!' Mrs Wiseman was too big to move quickly. She was floundering on the sofa. 'Oh, you horrible child. Marie, do something.'

The maid rushed towards her mistress and starting dabbing Mrs Wiseman with her apron, while Mr Wiseman stood fixed to the ground, watching in amused horror.

Rose looked up, then she did a terrible thing. She started to laugh and could not stop. The elegant, fragrant, opulent room she had entered was in uproar and filled with the smell of sick.

'She's hysterical! Marie, take the girl away.' Mr Wiseman was wondering if this had been such a good idea. He had persuaded his wife to take in the English girl.

'I know her father. Collects stamps,' he had told her. 'He's a gentleman, with a title, something to do with the Foreign Office. Think of it, dear, a name like ours, why, it wouldn't do any harm to show whose side we are on in this war.' Mr Wiseman was a businessman; he calculated the cost and benefit of everything. The price of the ruby necklace it took to convince his wife was a justified expense if it kept anti-German sentiment away from his business interests.

The Wisemans' house was symmetrical and orderly. A broad staircase went straight up from the middle of the hallway, did a ninety-degree turn at the wall and ended on a balcony landing with a wooden balustrade, before repeating the sequence up to the floor above.

'This floor's for the mister and missus,' explained Marie as they reached the first landing. 'Don't go here.' Marie turned to face Rose. She looked both scared and fierce.

Marie was about the same height as Rose, but her body was that of a will-o'-the wisp. Her maid's uniform hung off her such that when she walked, her clothes moved like a ghost skimming over the ground.

'This is your bathroom, miss,' said Marie, opening one of the doors on the upper landing. An enormous metal bathtub dominated the room. The biggest Rose had ever seen. There was a large white towel on a stand next to a basin and a flushing loo with a wooden throne for a seat. Rose stared in disbelief. What luxury!

'What shall I do?' she asked. 'I don't know what to do next.'

A little smile lit up Marie's face. She looked like a child. At sixteen, she was not much more than a child and had never known anything that someone else had not before. Marie put the plug in the bath, turned on the taps and felt the water with her hand as the bath filled up.

'Why don't you have a bath. Take those clothes off and in you get. I'll show you.' Quick as a flash, Marie pulled the black dress and dainty white apron over her head, hung them on the back of a chair and lowered herself into the bath. She squealed with delight and splashed the warm water over her face and arms.

The taste of sick was still in Rose's mouth. There was sick on her skirt. Her hysterical laughter had turned to quiet sobbing. She felt drained and dirty.

'Here I come,' she said, dumping her clothes on the floor in a heap and climbing over the edge of the bath. Marie splashed water at her. Rose splashed her back.

The water caressed their young bodies, one so very black and one so white.

'Having fun, girls?' It was Mr Wiseman. He was standing in the doorway watching them. Had he been there some time? Rose was not sure. She had been lost in the pleasure of play and laughter. He did not seem cross and was smiling indulgently at them. Marie looked terrified and slid further into the water, crossing her arms over her small breasts.

'She didn't know how to use the bath, sir. I showed her.' The words came out as a whisper.

'You sure did. You had better come and help your mistress now. I think she's the one in need of a bath.' Mr Wiseman laughed as if he had made a funny joke.

CHAPTER 7

Violet – A New Life

*T*he first few weeks at Holt Manor Billy Bob called, 'A bit barley wick and barley mow'. Vi had no idea what that meant. Billy Bob was absorbing country words as he breathed the air and stringing them together any which way. She supposed it was like the two ends of something; a good end and a bad end. There was certainly plenty of hard work to be done at the hard end, but alongside that, Vi loved the open space, the fields, the trees, the birds, the hedgerows.

Her favourite part of the day was strolling down the lane behind The Manor to Mr Turner's farm to collect the milk and the eggs. The September dew had turned the spider webs into intricate diamond patterns glistening on golden leaves. The sky went on forever. Vi had only ever glimpsed it between grimy grey walls before.

'How do,' said Mr Turner on her first visit. He reminded Vi of Mr Atkins, the rag-and-bone man, with his gruff voice and straightforward manner. Billy Bob gave her a nudge.

'Be nice to this one. He's got milk, he's got eggs …'

'Good morning, I'm Violet. Mrs Sproat sent me.' Polite with a smile, just like dealing with the church people.

It worked on Mr Turner. He looked Vi up and down slowly.

'From London, are you? One of those evacuees? You look like you could do with a bit of feeding. Tell Mrs Sproat I've put a couple of extra eggs in.' Mr Turner topped up the basket, where six pure white eggs lay protected by a golden bed of straw.

'Told you so,' shouted Billy Bob from the top of a stack of hay bales in the open barn.

Mrs Sproat had been surprised by the extra eggs and eyed Vi suspiciously.

'Not like Alf Turner to be generous. Did you steal them? Right or wrong, do they teach you that in London then? I don't know. You'd better boil up the water, make some tea and cook those eggs.'

Vi had scarcely spoken more than a few words to Mrs Sproat since she arrived despite an ongoing conversation. Mrs Sproat asked and answered all her own questions. She travelled from good to evil, self-pity to self-sacrifice and the ills of the world to the blessings that were to be had from it all without the need of anybody else.

'I'm not getting any younger. All those stairs and the mistress so incapacitated. Then they expect me to take in a young thief. Too good, that's me. Too kind-hearted and they all take advantage.'

In the midst of her sweeping declarations, she gave Vi instructions.

'Kettle on. Clean the grate. Peel the parsnips. Wash the plates.'

It was like a game. Vi quickly learnt to tune in to the relevant bits and ignore the rest. Her presence seemed a constant irritation to Mrs Sproat, so as soon as Vi completed all the tasks set for her she would slip off into the garden to find Billy Bob.

'Just stay round the back. Her Ladyship looks out the front, and I don't want you spoiling her view,' said Mrs Sproat, settling into her armchair for a snooze. She had more time for these now.

The back garden was a bit like the house, a series of different-shaped rooms. A cobbled courtyard with a row of disused stables led into a square walled garden with neat rows of vegetables and a netted fruit cage and beyond that an overgrown orchard. Billy Bob raced through the arched doorways set in the old stone walls that divided up the garden rooms.

'Look, Vi, apples! Pears! I don't know what this is, but try one.' Billy Bob tossed a dusty purple fruit at Vi. He took off the tweed cap he was wearing and started filling it with as much fruit as he could pick.

'It's a plum,' said Vi, biting into the juicy flesh.

Billy Bob could not stay still. He ran into the vegetable garden.

'Beans! This is where beans come from, Vi. And what's this?' Billy Bob pulled on a wispy green plant neatly placed in a row of identical wispy green plants.

'A carrot,' he announced, holding out a perfect orange carrot to Vi.

'What are you doing?'

The voice startled Vi. The carrot lay at her feet. Billy Bob had scarpered. A boy had come into the walled garden. He had a garden fork over his shoulder.

'I ain't done nothing,' said Vi. Big boys did not scare her, even really tall ones like this.

'I'm getting fresh air.'

'You're getting my carrots,' said the boy, lowering the fork and pointing it threateningly at Vi.

'Scram!' he said, jabbing the fork towards her.

'Shan't. I live here and you don't.' Billy Bob had crept up behind Vi. He was wearing long shorts and boxing gloves and was punching the air as he jumped up and down on the spot. No sign of the tweed cap.

'Stand your ground, Vi. He's a big lad. As he comes at you with the fork, duck then grab his legs. He'll topple, then you've got him.'

But the boy lowered the fork and stuck it into the soil before leaning on it and staring thoughtfully at Vi.

'I reckon you're that girl Dad talked about. Feisty one, aren't you. I do the veggies for The Manor. I take some for me and Dad and give the rest to Mrs S. So, as to who that carrot belongs to, well, I'm not sure.'

The boy bent down, picked up the carrot and snapped it in

half. He brushed the soil off the pointy end before handing it to Vi.

'Let's share,' he said. 'Mustn't let Mrs S catch us, though. *George Turner, you'll be the death of me! Eating all the carrots and here's me starving to death, fading away. There's a war on, you know.*'

It was a strange feeling for Vi to laugh. When had she last laughed? This boy, called George, had adopted perfectly Mrs Sproat's hunched form bunched with anger, and he was exactly mimicking her voice. The laugh felt good. The boy laughed too.

'George Turner at your service,' he said, putting his half of the carrot between his lips like a cigar and holding out his hand to Vi. She took it. His hand was bigger than hers and brown like a nut. It enveloped her slender fingers.

'Vi,' she said. 'Just Vi. Thank you for the carrot.'

George grinned back at her and took a big munch out of his carrot.

'Do you like horses? If we sneak a few carrots past old misery guts in there, we can take some down to the horses on the farm. They can't get enough of them.'

Vi nibbled the end of her carrot. It was as sweet as barley sugar.

'Don't really know any horses. Mr Atkins had one called Fred who pulled his cart, but I don't see him anymore …'

Vi's words tailed off. Her face took on its sullen stare. Why was she talking to him? What did he care?

The boy took no notice. He had started to dig up the carrots and was talking as much to himself as to Vi.

'One for the Sproat, one for the horses. Two for the Sproat, one for the horses. There's plenty here, she'll never know. How big are your pockets? I can stuff a couple in there and the rest up my shirt. I had better give her some beans too. Horses don't care much for beans.'

Vi looked across to where Billy Bob had settled on top of one of the spindly bean poles. The pole shook as he spoke.

'He knows everything, this one, doesn't he! *Have a carrot, Vi. My name's George, Vi.* Georgie Porgie, more like. *Look how strong I am, Vi.*'

There was a rhythmic metallic clunk as George's spade cut through the stony soil. A line of muddy carrots lay on the surface. A small trug sat waiting for them at the end of the row.

'Can I help you?' asked Vi, picking up the trug.

Billy Bob had disappeared.

George and Vi worked silently along the rows of carrots, easing each one gently out of the black soil.

'Er, yuk!' said Vi, throwing a perfectly formed carrot up in the air. George stuck his arm out and caught it.

'Howzat!

'It's just a worm,' said George, holding out the roots for Vi to see. 'When I was at school, the boys would dare each other to eat these. Ooh nice.' He lifted the wriggling worm towards his mouth.

'That's disgusting, Vi. He's a worm eater.' Billy Bob had appeared and was shielding Vi from the slaughter about to happen.

A robin settled on the handle of the trug, cocking his head towards the worm. The look of horror on Vi's face made George laugh.

'I'm not going to eat him, silly, but this little fellow will.' He placed the worm gently on the churned-up soil. 'Let's get these veggies to Mrs S and leave our friend here to his tea.'

'He's turned out all right, that George Turner,' said Mrs Sproat later as she and Vi peeled the carrots for supper. Vi let her continue. Hearing about George had a pleasant feel about it. She pictured his face laughing at her, but in a way that made her want to laugh too. Even Mrs S had smiled as George handed her the pile of vegetables as if presenting her with the Crown Jewels.

'His mum just upped and left when he was five. She'd always been a funny one. Too beautiful for her own good; she never settled on the farm, never took to being a mother. Stop gawping and keep peeling. That's enough chatter.'

Vi knew better than to ask questions. She applied herself to the vegetables and pictured George as a young boy sitting on the lap of his beautiful mother. How could he laugh like he did when he had lost something quite so special?

CHAPTER 8

Rose – In New York

There was nothing for Rose to do at the Wisemans'. Her room held no books, toys or games, just a high wooden double bed and a large wardrobe. Clothes, pretty clothes, hung in the wardrobe. A pale blue dress with a lacy white petticoat peeping out beneath the hemline and elaborate bows on the sleeves and around the neck, a similar dress in pink and another in yellow. Rose had rifled through these frothy creations on that first day until she found a red cotton sundress. There were no jodhpurs. She had tried to pull the dress over her head. Her arms got stuck. She could not move. Rose flung herself backwards onto the bed in an attempt to wriggle out of the red straitjacket. She felt a tugging.

'But your arms up straight, let me do it.' It was Marie who had come to fetch her for supper. 'I think that one's a bit small. Try this.' Marie handed Rose a blue serge skirt and white shirt. The skirt was a bit tight around Rose's tummy, but she allowed Marie to help her do up the buttons then followed the maid down the back stairs to the kitchen.

Each day, breakfast was brought to Rose in her room. Lunch was usually taken with Mrs Wiseman and her cohort of gossiping fellow wives, but supper was always in the kitchen with Marie and Maurice and quickly became the highlight of Rose's day. The kitchen was in the basement of the house and presided over by Monsieur Hugo, the chef, who spoke no English, only a stream of staccato French. Rose quickly learnt how to navigate her way through his empire, avoiding Monsieur Hugo, and make her way to the small parlour at the back with its pine table and chairs and the comforting presence of Marie and Maurice.

'*Et voila!*' Every evening, M. Hugo would land a steaming pot of stewed meat and vegetables in the centre of the table with a theatrical flourish.

'*Merci, monsieur,*' chorused Marie and Maurice while catching each other's eye as the chef left the room then bursting into giggles as he shut the door behind him. Then they would chatter like songbirds released from a cage.

'Things are not going well in England, Miss Rose,' said Maurice in his soft deep voice. He picked up his newspaper and showed Marie the headline: 'British Troops on the Run'. Maurice had wanted to know everything about England; what Rose ate, how the servants were treated and what Mr Churchill was really like. Rose answered his questions as best she could but realised how small her grasp on the world – outside her life with Mousie – was. After supper, they would play cards and Maurice taught her how to play backgammon, but Marie was at her happiest when Rose regaled them with stories of her outings with Mrs Wiseman.

If cosy evenings with Marie and Maurice were the best bit of Rose's day, mornings spent with Mrs Wiseman were the worst. Shoe-horned into one of the frilly dresses, Rose was expected to accompany the lady of the house to coffee mornings, lunches and *tête-à-têtes* with her many friends and acquaintances.

'We have taken her into the bosom of our family,' Mrs Wiseman would say, staring fondly at Rose. 'We felt it our duty to do our bit for the poor child.'

The ladies of New York's finest drawing rooms smiled indulgently at Rose. 'How lucky you are,' they would say. 'Have another cookie.'

The Mrs Wiseman who sat next to Rose in the car as they drove to these engagements was from a different mould. She never forgave Rose for being sick all over her.

'Don't speak unless you are spoken to. Don't slouch, and, for goodness' sake, smile a bit more.'

In the car mirror, Rose would see Maurice winking at her.

Knowing they would laugh about it later made these car journeys bearable for Rose. She started to put on a performance for Maurice's benefit.

'I will, Mrs Wiseman. Thank you, Mrs Wiseman. I am so grateful, Mrs Wiseman.

'Three bags full, Mrs Wiseman,' she added under her breath.

'What did you say? Stop muttering, girl. I can't stand muttering.'

'My heart is full of gratitude,' replied Rose, staring meekly down at her fur-lined boots, resisting a glance at the mirror.

'I am Wibbly Wobbly Wiseman's visible virtue,' she told Marie and Maurice.

'What does a visible virtue talk about?' asked Marie.

'I make it up most of the time. They all want to know about London and the war. I don't know anything,' Rose confessed. 'I don't even live in London. Yesterday, I had them listening.

'*My home has been reduced to rubble. My parents are in hiding. The Germans are expected any day.*

'That got me two bars of chocolate,' said Rose, rummaging in her pockets and handing Marie and Maurice a bar each.

'*My father is Mr Churchill's right-hand man. Mr C – as I called him – was a regular dinner guest. I used to sit on his knee and he would tell me stories about …*' Rose paused … '*elephants!*'

'Elephants?' Mrs Wiseman had been lapping up all the attention given to Rose, but even she baulked at elephants.

'It was a bit tricky to keep going with that one,' Rose told an enthralled Marie and Maurice, 'then I remembered Hannibal.

'*Mr C's hero is Hannibal and his elephants. That's his battle plan.* That's what I told 'em,' said Rose triumphantly. 'The ladies felt they should know about Hannibal, and all nodded like that made perfect sense.'

'You are a wicked girl, Miss Rose,' said Maurice, laughing so much he started hiccupping violently and had to be revived with a glass of water.

'Who is Hannibal?' asked Marie.

Of Mr Wiseman, Rose saw little. Maurice would drive him to his office downtown every morning and collect him in the evening or take him on to dinner with business colleagues. Mr Wiseman left it to his wife to show America whose side they were on in this war. That was until his wife refused to do so anymore.

The day had been like any other during the long cold winter Rose spent in New York. The snow in Central Park had melted and there was a faint hint of green on the trees as Maurice drove the woman and the child to their morning engagement. Rose had a tummy ache. She sat unnoticed in the corner of Hermione Hempel's drawing room, plaiting the fringe on one of her lampshades.

'What's that?' screamed Hermione as the social gathering came to an end and Rose was allowed to get up and follow Mrs Wiseman out of the room.

Rose turned and looked back at where she had been sitting and where the hysterical Hermione was now pointing. There was a circle of deep red blood on the silk chair cover and three drops of blood in a neat line linking the circle to Rose's retreating legs.

Rose felt dizzy. 'I don't know,' she said. The blood must be hers. She could feel a stickiness between her legs.

There was noise and fuss and agitation. It came to Rose from a distance. Mrs Wiseman propelled her from the room and out to the waiting car.

'She needs a rug, Maurice. Don't let her sit on the leather.'

It occurred to Rose that she might be dying and nobody seemed concerned.

When Mr Wiseman arrived home that evening, he was accosted by his wife in the hall. Rose heard shouting and went to the top of the stairs to listen.

'She's your responsibility. I want nothing more to do with her. Get her what she needs and tell her how to use it. I have had enough.' Mrs Wiseman jabbed at her husband's chest with a pudgy finger as she spoke. Then disappeared into the drawing room, slamming the door behind her. Rose heard Mr Wiseman calling for Marie.

That evening, as Rose was getting ready for bed, Mr Wiseman walked boldly into her bedroom, followed by a nervous-looking Marie who was carrying a stack of brown paper bags, a stretchy belt and some thick white pads. Mr Wiseman lowered his bulky body onto the bed beside Rose and picked up her hand.

'You're a woman now, Rose. Once a month, you will bleed like this. It's perfectly normal. Now Marie will show you how to deal with it.'

The little maid's hand was shaking as she held up the narrow belt and showed Rose where to place the pad so it sat between her legs.

'Then you clip the pad onto the belt. Afterwards, you put it in one of the bags and I will take it away.' Marie's voice was down to a whisper. What she was being forced to do in the presence of her employer was terrifying her.

'I don't want it. I don't want any of it,' shouted Rose, burying her head under the bedclothes. But Mr Wiseman was hurrying towards the door.

'You'll be fine. All perfectly normal,' he repeated. 'Leave her now, Marie.'

There was no one Rose could tell about the further visits of Mr Wiseman. He would appear in her room late at night and lie next to her under the covers. Rose lay rigid with fear, unable to utter a sound as he touched her body. One night, he did more than that; he hurt her. She cried out but he wedged his hand over her mouth and hissed,

'Shut up, you stupid girl!'

Maurice had lent Rose a book called *Uncle Tom's Cabin*. 'To help you to understand us,' he had said, handing her a battered copy and nodding at Marie. Words from the book stuck in

Rose's head: *I am braver than I was because I have lost all; and he who has nothing to lose can afford all risks.*

She bit down hard on Mr Wiseman's flabby hand. She was St George, plunging the sword into the dragon. Mr Wiseman recoiled.

'What the hell?'

Rose slipped from under him and out onto the narrow landing, slamming the door behind her. The doorframe shook. Rose ran down the flight of stairs to the main landing. She opened every door and closed each one with a crash. The whole house seemed to shake. The vibrations coursed through Rose and the shock waves woke the rest of the household. Mrs Wiseman emerged from her bedroom to see her husband on the upper landing. Marie appeared from the basement and stood looking up from the hallway below at the whirling dervish that was Rose. A final crash as Rose reached the door at the end of the landing. A Chinese vase stood on a stand alongside the door. Rose clasped the vase with both hands and raised it above her head before hurling it to the ground.

'No, Miss Rose,' she heard Marie shout.

The vase remained intact. Rose picked up the vase again and took it to the top of the main staircase. She watched as it bumped down each of the steps before crashing into pieces at the bottom.

Mrs Wiseman took in the scene before her. A look of disgust settled on her waxy, cream-covered face as she looked up at her dishevelled husband, motionless on the upper landing.

Maurice appeared alongside Marie in the hall.

Mrs Wiseman spoke slowly and with a dignity not assumed by her comic appearance.

'Maurice, I want you to get the car and take this girl to the people she met on her journey from England. She will stay there. Marie, pack her things. I never want to see her again.'

CHAPTER 9

Violet – Vi Dismounts

*T*ime stood still in mid-flight. That was what Vi learnt from her regular falls off Mousie's generous back; a moment of suspension when there was no going back and the certainty of pain that lay ahead. Rather like being sick.

George had insisted she learn to ride without a saddle or bridle, just a simple rope head collar.

'You'll learn to stay on then you can ride anything,' he told her, but it seemed to Vi that all she learnt was how to fall off.

Mr Turner had suggested the riding lessons. Vi had been sorting jars in the pantry when she heard him in the kitchen, an unexpected visitor. She peered through the half-open door. He had taken his cap off and was holding it awkwardly in his fist. He seemed rooted to the back-door mat.

'I reckon it will do that young lass good, and it will give George something to focus on. The pony too; doesn't do a horse any good to be left alone, probably go feral.'

Vi could hear Mrs Sproat pounding the bread she was making. *Slap! Slap!* – getting louder.

'You'd get more out of her if she had a bit of fun.' Mr Turner had obviously come to say his piece and was not going to let the thwack of dough put him off his stride.

'I'll have to check with Her Ladyship and if the girl starts slacking, well—'

'You won't regret it.' Mr Turner did not let Mrs Sproat finish. It seemed he could not get out of the kitchen fast enough.

Beyond saying 'Put it there' when Vi took Lady Symes her breakfast every morning, her mistress had shown no interest in Vi, so she would not be much of a hurdle to overcome. Riding lessons! With George! It took Vi several seconds to manipulate the smile on her face and emerge into the kitchen with an everyday scowl in place.

Vi's excitement was short-lived. Mousie had not been ridden for some time and had no intention of being caught.

'Approach him slowly from the side and slip the head collar over his head,' George instructed Vi.

'Don't listen to him, Vi.' Billy Bob had appeared alongside Vi as she gingerly made her way towards the quietly grazing pony.

'He's out to make a fool of you.'

Vi lunged at the pony with the rope. It slid off his head as he trotted away from her across the field. Vi followed after him, determined to show George she was not scared, but each time it was the same. She got close and the pony would toss his mane and move away.

'He's laughing at you. Look!' Billy Bob pointed at George standing by the gate with a big grin on his face.

'Stupid horse!' Vi threw the head collar to the ground. As she walked away, her foot got caught in the trailing rope and Vi tumbled onto the muddy grass.

'I'm sorry,' said George, coming across to give her a helping hand up. 'Look, I'll show you how to do it.' He rattled a bowl of food and called out to the pony. 'Come on, Mousie. Enough, old friend.'

In the weeks that followed, Vi often looked back at that day and thought how easily she could have given up. Sticking with something was new for Vi.

'Take the rough with the smooth,' George told Vi. 'You have to fall off at least seven times before you become a rider.'

Vi lost count of how many tumbles she had, but each time she got back on and her balance grew better. She got used to the pony's bouncy stride and his sudden stops to nibble a leafy branch. In one ear, she had the entreaties of Billy Bob.

'He's out to kill you. We need to get out of here.'

And in the other was George encouraging her to sit tall and hang on.

Vi did hang on. She hung on to the pony, to the busy routine of her new life and to every word George uttered. He took to riding his father's cob, Blossom, and the two riders would head off into the woods as spring was beginning to make itself felt.

'Look at that big house,' said Vi on one such ride, pointing across a low hedge at a stately manor house set in open parkland.

'My dad worked there before he got the farm tenancy. It was Sir Percy's place then. I think it's a school now. He met my mother there.' George had never mentioned his mother to Vi.

'Yes, look, there's a group of girls, over there, playing cricket,' he continued hastily. 'Come on, let's go before they see us.'

But Vi was staring at the girls. Before George could stop her, she had turned through a gap in the hedge and was cantering towards the cricketers. Billy Bob had jumped up behind her on Mousie's back and was egging Vi on, delighted at the turn of events.

All the girls looked up as the thundering hooves approached.

'Pamela!' Vi called out, waving frantically at the girl holding the cricket bat. 'It's me.'

'It's the girl from the train,' shouted one of the smaller cricketers as Vi drew alongside them. Mousie came to a sudden halt.

'Oh, we wondered what happened to you,' said Pamela, dropping the bat and rushing forward to greet Vi. 'I remember you in my prayers every night. Did someone come to meet you?'

'Yes,' said Vi triumphantly. Pamela looked so happy to see her. 'I was met and I work in a big house, not as big as this, and I have a friend and he takes me riding.'

George had ridden up to where the girls clustered around Vi. 'We can't be here, Vi,' he said. There was a shout from the house. Miss Stretton had appeared at the front door.

'Oops, yes, you'd better go. Come and see us again,' said Pamela. 'Come for tea.'

Vi followed George back through the hedge. 'What was all

that about?' he asked. 'You're going to get us into terrible trouble.' George had not been cross with Vi since the incident with the carrot. Vi did not care. All she could hear was the delight in Pamela's voice on seeing her again and the pride in her own as she related her new life to her erstwhile train companions.

'Race you back,' she yelled at George as she turned for home.

Vi gave herself an unassailable lead and emerged triumphantly from the wood above the farm. She was mid-flight over the small log George had taught her to jump when she saw a girl in the middle of the farm track. There was the face from the silver frame on Lady Symes' dressing table. A black and white face that was now various shades of pink. Rose. George's reaction confirmed it.

'Get off, Vi. Just get off.'

'A big pink blancmange,' said Billy Bob, taking Vi's hand and leading her away from the pony. 'No danger in a blancmange.'

'You'll be too big for him now,' said Vi, throwing her riding crop to the ground in front of Rose.

'Look out, Vi!' Billy Bob ducked as Rose picked up the riding crop and started hitting out at Vi. 'Run, Vi, run.'

Mrs Sproat was sitting at the kitchen table with her head in her hands when Vi reached the house. A telegram was open on the table in front of her. She looked up as Vi came in.

'She's back then. Didn't want her in America either by the sound of it. All those young men dying and Little Miss Madame sails away and sails on back again without a hair on her precious head unsettled.'

Vi surprised herself and put her arm around Mrs Sproat's slumped shoulders. She had never so much as touched her before, but the housekeeper seemed crushed. Over the months Vi had been at The Manor, there had been a change in Mrs Sproat. She moaned less and laughed more. Vi had felt a glimmer of warmth grow between them that seemed to unfurl along with the leaves on the fruit trees. Mrs Sproat had let Vi take some of Rose's clothes, but she would never be drawn on the absent girl.

'Best off without her,' was all she would say, pursing her lips before handing Vi washing to hang out or pans to clean. George was the same. Speculation about Miss Rose was out of bounds in their conversation. He would not speak ill of her, and Vi was aware of some unseen loyalty to Mousie's mistress. This had only served to add to Vi's fascination with this girl, whose life she was increasingly inhabiting.

Her first foray into Rose's room had been to collect some clothes as instructed, but Vi sneaked back there whenever she could, spreading herself out on the rose- strewn eiderdown, calling to Billy Bob through the open window to marvel at 'Miss Violet and her boudoir'.

Mrs Sproat let Vi's arm hang briefly over her shoulders before hauling herself out of the chair.

'You had better take those boots off and come and help me make up Miss Rose's bed.'

Making up a bed had become one of Vi's favourite tasks. She liked folding the edge of a crisp white bedsheet into a sharp point before deftly creating what Mrs Sproat called 'a hospital corner' and tucking it underneath the mattress to hold the sheet in place.

'I don't want her making my bed.' Rose came into the bedroom as Mrs Sproat and Vi smoothed down the top sheet. 'I don't want her touching any of my things.'

'Now come, Miss Rose, this is Violet. She has been helping me since the war started. It's not been easy, you know. We can't all run away.'

Vi kept her head down as Mrs Sproat addressed the angry girl. She was not sure how to deal with the sudden arrival of Miss Rose. There was no doubt Vi had been wearing her clothes, riding her pony and living in her house. Vi had no right to any of it. She felt herself back in the church, taking crumbs from the ladies and gentlemen. There was only one thing to do.

'Yes, Miss Rose. I am sorry if I have been presumptuous. It won't happen again.' Vi smiled the gentlest of smiles and gave a little bob of her legs.

'Get out!' shouted Rose.

Vi bobbed again and walked towards the door, casting a sideways glance at a surprised Mrs Sproat as she went.

CHAPTER 10

Rose – Rose Returns

The boat trip back to England from America had been no fun for Rose. She had been restricted to her cabin by the surly purser who had received her on board, and by unrelenting seasickness. Even without those restrictions, it had been made clear to Rose that the troop ship she was on was no place for a child.

David and Aubrey's Uncle Arthur had arranged Rose's passage home.

'He has friends in the right places,' David told her when the plan was announced.

Both he and Aubrey had been surprised and delighted to find Rose had suddenly turned up at their uncle's house. They had been asleep when she arrived. Mrs Mac answered the door to Maurice's insistent knocking.

'Rose! What on earth has happened?' Mrs Mac bustled Rose inside while Maurice stood helplessly on the doorstep.

'You need to take her. I'll leave her trunk on the step,' Rose heard him say. 'She's not safe.' Mrs Mac held Rose close. Rose was shaking.

'Thank you,' said Mrs Mac quietly.

The weeks at Uncle Arthur's house passed in a blur for Rose. Aubrey wanted to show her everything in his new life; the enormous bedroom all to himself, the train set with its own room too and the house cat, Soots, and David wanted to know all about the man who collected stamps.

'Give her time,' was all Mrs Mac would say when Rose stared bleakly back at the two boys. Rose felt removed from everything around her, as if she could not resurface to join them. She did not respond to Mrs Mac's gentle probing but shuddered every time the Wisemans were mentioned.

'We need to get you home,' Mrs Mac told her. 'She'll be better off with her family,' Rose heard her telling the boys.

'But what's wrong with her?' demanded Aubrey.

'Just leave her be,' said Mrs Mac.

Rose had remained numb to everything until she got home and saw the girl riding Mousie. All that had happened to Rose, all that she had not understood and all that she had understood too well came together in a great ball of hatred directed at the girl.

'Why is she here?' Rose shouted at her mother, who had shrunk even further into her chaise longue while Rose had been away. She seemed exhausted by Rose's return, only managing to sit up briefly, wave a lace handkerchief at her daughter and exclaim, 'Oh, my darling, you survived!' before collapsing back into her cushions.

'Times are hard,' Lady Symes went on. 'It's not like America; we have all been struggling.' Lady Symes took a deep breath as if recovering from a long speech and summoning energy for another one. 'Mrs Sproat needed help. Violet's a good maid. We gave her a home when she was desperate. Now I must rest, my darling girl. So wonderful to have you home. When I am feeling stronger, you must tell me all about your adventures.'

Rose spent the first few days back at Holt Manor in her room. She curled up under the bedcovers and slept. Mrs Sproat brought food up on a tray, but Rose had no appetite. Sometimes, she got out of bed and briefly sat by the window. She could make out George working in the vegetable garden. When the sun came out, Mrs Sproat and the girl appeared with a basket of washing. Rose could see they worked well together. The girl would bend and pick up the clothes and Mrs Sproat pegged them on the line. Vi made Mrs Sproat laugh when she pointed and said something as a couple of ducks waddled by. George must have heard them and, leaving his spade, joined them by the washing line. Rose turned away and hid herself under the covers. That girl had to go.

It was a nugget of an idea that finally raised Rose from her bed with a purpose. She went over to the top drawer of her dressing table and took out a soft black velvet pouch. 'You'll do nicely,' she said, pulling out a single strand of creamy pearls. The card Aunt Maud had written came out with them: *To my Niece on the occasion of her Christening from Aunt Maud.*

A totally useless present Rose had believed – until now. Rose put her freshly washed jodhpurs on, ate the lunch Mrs Sproat had left for her and put her plan into action. First, Rose had to wait for the girl to appear in the garden – she seemed to be chatting animatedly to someone, but there was no one about – then on to the second stage. Rose trod lightly up the stairs to the girl's room and placed the pearls in their velvet pouch under the girl's pillow. Then, skipping downstairs, she let herself out of the front door and went to see her pony.

Mr Turner was sweeping the yard when she arrived.

'Feeling better?' he asked Rose. She stopped herself from snapping back at him, *There's nothing wrong with me!*

'I'm fine, thank you. I have come to ride Mousie. If that's okay. I wondered if ... I'm not too big for him now, am I?'

Mr Turner looked her up and down. 'I think he'll do you for a bit longer yet. If you get him in and saddle him up, I can give you a quick lesson, get your horse legs working again.'

'Thank you. I'd like that.'

'Didn't work out for you then in America?'

Rose swayed slightly. Mr Turner put his hand out to stop her falling.

'There were no horses. No fresh air. I needed fresh air.' Rose steadied herself and smiled reassuringly at the farmer. He would understand horses and fresh air.

It was wonderful to be back on Mousie. Rose forgot every-thing as she moved up and down rhythmically to his bouncy trot and followed Mr Turner's instructions, weaving a circle around him in the corner of an empty field. She wasn't too big for Mousie, the girl would be gone soon and her life would go back as it was.

Rose had not expected to find her father's car on the drive when she returned to the house. He must have known she was back. It was unlikely he would be pleased. The front door creaked loudly as she opened it. A quiet entrance was impossible, but it made no difference, for there he was, standing in the middle of the hallway smiling benignly and addressing Mrs Sproat and the girl.

'Mrs Sproat tells me you are settling in well and working hard.'

'Thank you, sir.'

'There'll be more to do now my daughter's back.' He turned towards the creaking door. 'Ah, there you are.' Sir Reginald did not have a smile for Rose.

'I get a telegram from some unknown Arthur Wilson in New York telling me you are on your way back. No explanation. There's a war on and you see fit to swan back and forth across the Atlantic when everybody else has got much better things to do.'

Her father's presence had been a shock to Rose, but it was dawning on her that if she played her cards right, his arrival could be beneficial to her plan. She bent down to remove her dusty boots.

'I need to wash and change. I'll talk to you at dinner, Father.' Rose picked up the boots and held them out towards the girl. 'These need cleaning.' The girl did not take them. Rose dropped them at the girl's feet. 'I'll need some hot water too.' With as much composure as Rose could muster, she made her way up the main staircase, each fall of her socked feet drumming into her that when the worst has already happened, nothing has the power to hurt.

Rose had no intention of joining her father for dinner, but she dressed as if she did. She found a dress in her cupboard that just about fitted her. It was tight over her chest and rounded tummy. There was not much she could do with her hair, but tying it back with a ribbon gave an air of trying.

'Right, here we go,' said Rose to her mirrored reflection. Best to work on her mother first; Lady Symes could make a drama out of a pin dropping. Rose ran along the passageway to her mother's room then charged through the door shrieking, 'They've gone! My pearls have gone. We've been burgled. The burglars may still be in the house.'

Lady Symes screamed in a very satisfactory way, sufficient to summon her husband.

'For goodness' sake, control yourself, woman.'

'It's the Germans, they're here.' Lady Symes clutched the pearl choker around her delicate neck. 'We'll be murdered in our beds.'

Sir Reginald turned to his daughter. 'What have you done to upset your mother? Hardly back in the house and you're causing trouble.'

'It's my pearls, Father, the ones from Aunt Maud, they are missing. I was going to wear them for dinner.'

'This is ridiculous. If we'd had burglars, they would have taken a lot more than a set of pearls.'

'I don't know, Father. The new maid has been in my room while I was away. She took my clothes. Maybe ...'

CHAPTER 11

Violet – Vi Runs Away

It took Vi several seconds to take in the scene before her. Then she ran. She ran down both sets of stairs, across the hall and out of the front door. Billy Bob was waiting, dressed in prison overalls with a swag bag tossed over his shoulder. He took Vi's hand.

'It was never going to work,' he said, pulling her down the drive and out onto the road.

'I need to stop for a moment, get my breath back.' Vi flung herself into the dry ditch beside the verge and lay there breathing heavily.

'They were all in my room, not Mrs Sproat, but she had told me to go up there, said I was needed. Even Her Ladyship was there. Sir Reginald was holding Miss Rose's pearls. I know those pearls. I've seen them in her drawer, but I never touched them. They were all staring at me. I can't go back. Miss Rose was sort of smiling. It was horrible.'

The sun was setting across the fields. Billy Bob peered down at Vi. 'We need to find somewhere to shelter for tonight. We'll make a plan in the morning.'

'We can't go to the farm; they'll think I'm a thief. Why wouldn't they? Pamela! What about Pamela? She wanted to see me. We can go through the woods. I think I can find the school again.'

It was dark by the time they reached the school, its bulky outline unmistakable in the gloom, a tiny chink of light from a lower window where the blackout curtain was not doing its job. Billy Bob and Vi peered through the gap. There were girls sprawled around the room reading books and lounging on large floral sofas.

'There's a pavilion on the lawn. I saw it when we rode here. We can hide there,' said Vi. Billy Bob nodded and solemnly offered Vi his arm so he could escort her across the grass down to the cricket pavilion.

The pavilion was just a single room filled with hastily stacked chairs, piles of tennis racquets, a heap of tartan rugs, a croquet set and one long wooden bed- like chair that had seen better days. Vi wrapped herself in some of the rugs, took a cricket pad for a pillow and curled up on the long chair. She wanted to make sense of what had happened. It had been terrible for her when Rose came back so unexpectedly from America. Vi knew her life at The Manor would change, but as the days had gone by, she had accepted that. She still saw George every day, and although Mrs Sproat had become even more bad-tempered, it was mostly not directed at Vi.

'They'll be sending her off to boarding school, I reckon,' Mrs Sproat had told Vi. 'Nobody wants her here.'

So Vi had decided to put up with the poisonous Miss Rose and hope she would be gone again before too long, but now this.

It was not difficult to catch Pamela's attention in the morning. All the girls spilled out of the school in their hats and coats, laughing and chatting, with Miss Stretton leading the way.

'Come along, girls, breathe. Get those lungs working. Healthy body, healthy mind.' The headmistress was marching like a soldier. Billy Bob was marching alongside her in full military uniform with a row of shiny medals. As Pamela crossed in front of the pavilion, Vi rolled a cricket ball out of a narrow gap in the door to land at Pamela's feet. In a single, almost imperceptible, movement, Pamela scooped up the ball, glanced at the door and turned away from her companions.

'I'm just going to check we've got enough bats for later. I'll catch you up,' said Pamela.

Billy Bob stopped marching and whistled through his teeth. 'What a girl!'

'Goodness! Vi, what are you doing here?' Vi stood in the centre of the room as Pamela entered. She stepped forward and engulfed Pamela in a hug.

'I didn't know where else to go.'

Pamela listened while Vi related all that had happened.

'… but I didn't touch them. I don't know how they got there. You must believe me.'

'Of course I do,' said Pamela gently. 'I have to go before anyone misses me. Wait here and I'll try and bring you some food later, and we can see what's to be done.'

'Don't tell anyone,' begged Vi. 'They'll put me in prison and it's not my fault.'

A bell rang. Pamela hurried away.

Vi picked her way around her new abode and found a large musty parasol, faded with age and enjoyed by moths. She angled it across one of the corners to give herself a space to hide in with a well-placed moth-made spyhole to check on visitors. She scoured about for food but found none. Billy Bob was sitting on the wooden veranda outside. He had changed into cricket whites and was sporting a jaunty striped cap.

'Rose must have really hated me to do that.'

'You were in her way, simple,' said Billy Bob with a shrug. 'She was jealous.'

'Of me!' said Vi. 'She's got everything. What have I got?'

'Well, she wanted you gone, that's for sure.'

'And I am gone,' said Vi quietly.

True to her word, Pamela came back in the afternoon, but she had obviously been unable to shake off her friends. They burst into the pavilion behind Pamela.

'Did you hear what he said, Pam? It was that boy, wasn't it, the one on the horse?'

'What did he want with Miss Stretton?'

Through her small peephole, Vi watched as Pamela gathered her friends around her on Vi's erstwhile bed. Pamela glanced around the room, her eyes alighting briefly on the parasol. In a loud conspiratorial whisper, she said,

'It was that boy. He was looking for Vi, the girl from the train. He told Miss Stretton she'd gone missing and had anybody seen her? Miss Stretton didn't really know what he was on about, but the boy kept talking.'

'Had she run away?' asked one of the girls, enthralled by Pamela's eavesdropping ability.

'I didn't hear everything. There was something about a missing necklace, but they know Vi didn't take it. The house-keeper had seen it in its rightful place when she'd put away some clothes that afternoon. There was no way Vi could have taken it. They want her to go back. They want to say sorry, but they don't know where she is.' Pamela said the last bit very loudly in the direction of the parasol.

'I wouldn't go back,' said one of the girls.

'Me neither,' said another. 'They sound horrid people.'

'But that boy wants her to go back. He cares enough to go looking for Vi. Like a knight errant. It' so romantic,' sighed a girl, leaning dreamily back on Vi's knee pad pillow.

Pamela laughed. 'Well, let's hope he finds her then. Come on, we had better go.'

Vi peered out from behind her parasol. All was quiet. A neatly wrapped newspaper package had been left under one of the chairs. Inside was a square of jam sandwiches. Pamela had been true to her word. It reminded Vi of the church ladies and their dainty offerings. Perhaps she should try and get back to London, to her mother and the life she had left behind. She wasn't sure she could face them at Holt Manor despite all she had heard Pamela say. The newspaper wrapping had a picture of the King and Queen on the front. They were picking their way over rubble tumbled in uneven heaps alongside the jagged remains of a wall incongruously covered in pink roses.

Royal couple visit the people of the East End where the relentless German bombing has led to countless lives lost and homes destroyed.

Vi read on. Could her mother have survived this onslaught? This is what Vi's mother had saved her from by telling Vi to leave London. She had sent her away because she cared, and now George wanted her back because he cared. Vi bit into the soft sandwich. Pamela cared too. It was an odd moment, an odd place to feel loved, but Vi did.

To err is human, to forgive divine. Where had Vi heard those words before? She went outside to share them with Billy Bob.

'We're going back,' she told him. 'No, not to London, to The Manor. I didn't do anything wrong.'

'Georgie Porgie comes looking and you go all *forgive us our trespasses*,' was all Billy Bob could find to say.

Rose was grooming Mousie in the yard as Vi emerged from the woods behind the farm. Mr Turner saw her first.

'You're back, lass. I'm glad to see you. George, she's here,' he shouted towards the barn. 'Come on, miss,' he said to Rose, taking the brush gently out of her hand. 'You need to apologise.'

But it was Vi who approached Rose. She walked straight up to her and took both Rose's hands in hers.

'It's okay.'

Rose had been sullenly staring at her feet. She looked up in surprise at Vi's quiet words. How wretched she looked, thought Vi. Rose's hands were clammy and shook slightly, as if searching for a firm hold.

'You don't look well,' said Vi. 'I'll help you back to the house. George, here, give me a hand.'

George and his father were looking on in amazement. This was not a scene they had ever imagined. But the girl did look peaky. A memory came back to Mr Turner: his beautiful wife when she was expecting George, the early days with the sickness, the pallor and the slightly swollen belly. He needed to speak to Mrs Sproat.

Rose allowed Vi to lower her onto the stone mounting block. 'I'm sorry,' she mumbled. 'It was a terrible thing to do. I am glad you are back. I was so worried something might have happened to you, and it was all my fault.'

Billy Bob plonked himself down alongside Rose. 'No one cares for her,' he said, looking up at Vi. 'Not even Georgie Porgie.'

CHAPTER 12

Rose – Expectations

'*A*re you awake, Vi?'
A muffled sound came from the end of the narrow bed.

'I'm scared, Vi. You will stay with me, won't you? When it happens.'

The two girls lay top to toe in the bed. When they first arrived at the nursing home, they had lain side by side, but Rose's increasing girth had pushed Vi further and further to the edge, so they had switched to each end. Rose's sleep was intermittent as the baby tossed and turned inside her. Vi's steadying hand in the yard all those months ago had become Rose's permanent rock and she clung to it.

'I'm here, Rose. I'm not going anywhere. We'll do this together, like I said. Is it moving a lot?'

'Not too bad.'

'Well get some sleep then.'

It was Mrs Sproat who had made everything happen. Mrs Sproat, who hated Rose as much as Rose hated her. After the furore over the necklace, everyone had wanted Vi back and Rose sent away again, this time to boarding school. But Vi had forgiven Rose and something had changed in Mrs Sproat.

'Have you had your monthlies recently?' Mrs Sproat asked Rose while bringing in her breakfast. Both she and Vi had fussed over Rose since Vi's return a few days earlier. Rose had forgotten all about the bleeding she had in America. It had not happened again and Rose had certainly not missed it. Mrs Sproat sat down on Rose's bed. The housekeeper's face was unusually soft and sad. She fixed her eyes on her own swollen ankles.

'Did something happen in America, Miss Rose? Why did they send you back so suddenly? Was there a man? Did he do something to you? Perhaps someone on the boat …?'

Mrs Sproat's cousin Enid had got in the family way when she was fourteen. The two cousins had been inseparable, but one day Enid wasn't there anymore. Her pretty, vivacious cousin had become increasingly wretched then simply disappeared, with no word spoken of her again. It was only snippets of whispered gossip – 'she's no better than she ought to be … girls like that … she'll go to one of them homes … the baby'll have to go' – that helped the young Mrs Sproat piece together what had happened. She had always felt guilty about Enid and wished she could have done more for her, looked for her even.

'You have to tell me, Miss Rose. I can help you. I think you are expecting.'

Expecting what? Rose stared blankly at Mrs Sproat. It was making her uncomfortable having the older woman sitting beside her and being kind. Then she placed her hand on Rose's tummy.

'Alf Turner spotted it. Strange for a man to notice anything, but I suppose he's seen lots of lambs and calves.'

Had Mrs Sproat gone mad? Expecting a calf? What was she on about?

'You're having a baby, Miss Rose, and by my reckoning in about four months. But you listen to me; I don't care what anyone tells you, this is not your fault.'

There was unexpected vehemence in Mrs Sproat's voice. Rose had grown accustomed to everything being her fault. But a baby, how was that possible?

It was as if an alien creature was inside her body and of course it was Rose's fault. Vi came into the room to collect Rose's breakfast tray. She was humming a tune that sounded like the one they always sung at harvest time about ploughing and seed scattering. Rose had watched Vi earlier coming up to the house with George and the milk and eggs. The two of them had been laughing. Did they know about the creature inside Rose? Was that what they were laughing at? Vi obviously did. She sat down on Rose's bed and picked up Rose's hand.

'It's going to be okay. I can look after you, can't I, Mrs S? You will need lots of food. Could be difficult with rationing but we'll manage. I can get you clothes. They will have to be bigger ones, but we can go to the church jumble and then Mrs Sproat can make them fit you. People had babies all the time in London. They were sweet, but sometimes they coughed a lot and got ill. Yours won't, not here,' she added hastily.

'What are you prattling on for?' said Mrs Sproat, but she was smiling at Vi. There was something rather cosy about the three of them sitting on the bed. Rose squeezed Vi's hand.

'Thank you,' said Rose. Vi's hand felt strong and warm.

'It's not going to be easy,' said Mrs Sproat. I need to think it through and make a plan. Leave it with me and we will not say anything to your parents yet. You two go off to the church hall this morning, and I will try and conceal things a bit longer.'

At the back of the church hall were rows of shelves piled high with a motley selection of old clothes: shirts, moth-eaten jumpers, stained waistcoats and uncoupled shoes. A clothes rail had been placed in front of the shelves where a three-piece suit and a limp tea dress hung.

'They look like a courting couple,' said Vi, picking up one of the suit sleeves.

'Good day to you, madame.' Vi shook the sleeve of the dress. 'Would you care to dance?'

Rose grabbed the dress and held it against her. 'I'm frightfully sorry, sir, I can't. I am far too busy.' Rose twirled the dress in a pirouette across the empty hall. 'I'm having a baby, you see.'

Vi stared at Rose for a moment. Then they both burst out laughing.

'Come on! This is going to be fun,' said Vi, picking up an enormous pair of Oxford bags. 'Mrs S will knock up an outfit from each leg of these.'

It was easy to forget about the baby when Vi was around. Rose took to having her breakfast with Vi and joining her on the daily trip to the farm. George seemed uncomfortable around Rose and looked away when he spoke to her. Years of subservience prevented the cosy relationship he seemed to have with Vi. For Rose, it was enough to be with them both. She helped Vi with her chores, freeing them up to visit Mousie in the afternoon. Rose took one of her pony books down to the yard.

'Look, here's how to prepare for a gymkhana,' Rose showed Vi. 'We can make our own and you can ride Mousie and I'll be the judge. George, we need buckets and poles.'

But, despite the fun, Rose's tummy kept on swelling and, unbeknownst to Rose, a plan was being hatched. Only once it was all sorted did Vi explain it to her, and only when it was put into action did Rose actually believe such an extraordinary thing could happen.

'You had a nanny when you were born,' Vi told her. 'Nurse Primrose. She was here for a few years then went to Brighton and set up a nursing home. Mrs S has kept in touch and she's arranged for you to go there to have the baby.' Vi seemed very pleased with this arrangement and beamed at Rose. 'I'm coming with you!'

'Then what?' demanded Rose. 'What about Father and Mother? They may not notice me but they'll notice a baby.' Vi looked even more pleased.

'All sorted.'

And it was. Mrs Sproat had spoken to Alf Turner first.

'The baby will come back to the farm as Vi's,' she told him.

'Why? And why on earth should we have anything to do with it?'

'Because George will be the father. Because you are going to get the deeds to the farm in return for your help and your silence.'

'Ah, I see you have thought it all through. Sir Reginald will hand over the farm just like that … we'll take in a bastard child and everything in the garden will be rosy!'

'It won't be a bastard. George and Vi can get married in a few years. Nobody notices these things with a war on. And anyway, what if the war goes on and on? George will be called up. What will you be left with then? Think it through, Alf Turner. Vi's a good worker. You can have a woman in your house again to look after you both, and young life when so much young life is dying.'

'And the farm? That lot don't give away land, and I don't give away my son to some ridiculous scheme.'

Mrs Sproat left Mr Turner to think over what she had said and then, according to Vi, had turned her attention to Sir Reginald. Getting him down from London hadn't been easy, but a telegram announcing a serious decline in his wife's health and her possible imminent death had done the trick.

'She seems fine to me, and Dr Randall says there is no change in her condition. I have important work in London, Mrs Sproat. There is a war on.'

'It's Miss Rose we need to talk about. I didn't think you'd come for her.'

'My secretary is looking into boarding schools. She's nothing but trouble, stop wasting my time.'

'She's having a baby. You sent her halfway round the world to be molested by a man whom you would have called a gentleman. Rose is still a child, your child, and you have to take responsibility. If you don't, I will make sure everyone knows what has happened. What you have done and what your so-called friend has done. I can help you or I can expose you.'

'This sounds like blackmail, Mrs Sproat.'

'I suppose it is, sir.'

Rose had been incredulous as Vi explained how Mrs Sproat had gone about making everything all right. Sir Reginald had not given in easily. Alf Turner had been right; holding on to land was rule number one of the landed gentry.

'Or perhaps rule number two after avoiding scandal,' said Vi. 'And as for Mr Turner and George, I think it was just kindness in the end, that and the chance to have their own farm.'

Rose lay in the narrow bed where, despite everything, she felt calm, more calm than she ever remembered feeling. The anger had gone; that's what it was. Vi was going to look after her, 'and you,' she said quietly to her unborn child.

CHAPTER 13

Violet – Vi's Plan

Vi did not tell Rose how George felt about the plan. The kitchen had been warm and cosy with a bubbling pan of soup on the range and a tray of freshly baked biscuits cooling on the table when Mrs Sproat laid out before Vi the plan she had made for Miss Rose and the baby. To Vi, it was like hearing a new fairy story, complete with witch and cauldron.

'… George will come back from the war when it's over – it will be over one day – then he'll marry you, and the baby will be brought up by the two of you on the farm.' Mrs Sproat was not given to theatrical flourishes, but there was a definite spreading of her hands and a vigorous nod of her head as the housekeeper ended her speech.

'And we'll live happily ever after, I suppose,' said Vi.

'Well, yes!' said Mrs Sproat triumphantly.

'What does George think?'

'Ah yes, well, Alf – Mr Turner – and I thought you might explain it all to him.' Mrs Sproat's words tailed off. 'Here, take him a biscuit. I think he's in the garden. I'm sure he'll see the sense in it.'

Vi doubted he would for a moment.

'Alf Turner won't agree unless George is happy, so you make sure you give it to him straight, all the advantages. He's a kind lad.'

The back door was open onto the courtyard. Billy Bob leant against the doorframe, never quite inside.

'The old girl's gone mad! The Gorgeous Porgeous is to take on Miss Princess Rosamunda's baby and you into the bargain. We have been in some pickles, Vi, but this is the pickliest of them all. Don't jump into it.'

Billy Bob was dressed as a judge, complete with wig and gown. Just like the judge in *Alice in Wonderland*. Vi wasn't jumping; she was falling down a rabbit hole where nothing made sense.

'Well, let's see, shall we?' Vi scooped up a couple of biscuits, tipped Billy Bob's wig over his eyes and ran into the garden.

She found George sweeping leaves along the nut walk.

'I've got biscuits. You look like you could do with a break,' said Vi. George was always hungry. He looked so pleased to see her. Perhaps they could have a life together. Or was it just the biscuits?

They sat down to eat their biscuits on the stone bench set into the wall. Billy Bob perched above them. The whole plan tumbled out of Vi, from Rose's pregnancy to the handing-over of the farm. Each time she took a breath, Billy Bob would add '… and then … and then…'

The stillness of the garden after Vi's torrent of words was loud in its emptiness.

'Say something,' said Vi eventually. George had not moved the entire time she had been speaking.

'Sounds like it's all sorted.' George picked up his broom and fell into the rhythmic swoosh of dried leaves.

'That went well,' said Billy Bob. 'Wreck a man's life as easy as that.' He ran alongside George, singing in time to the brush-strokes.

> *'Getting a baby,*
> *Getting a wife,*
> *Getting a farm,*
> *Losing a life.'*

Vi ignored Billy Bob. She ran down the path and stood blocking George's way.

'Please talk to me, George. Think about the farm and us being together. We can make it work.'

George continued his brushing in a sweep around her. He did not look up.

'They think I'm going to get killed, Vi. That's what this is all about, don't you see? I don't come back from the war, everything works out for them; no disgrace for the Symes family, the baby down as mine so will inherit the farm when Dad goes, then they claim baby and farm back as their own. Bingo! All's well again. It's not happy families they are looking at, Vi, and really it's got nothing to do with me.'

'He's not buying it, Vi. Georgie Porgie, the Farmer's Son, is not playing.'

Vi did not see George again before she and Rose left for the clinic. Sir Reginald sent his chauffeur to take them. The chauffeur kept his eyes down, his face impassive as he loaded the bags and held the car door open while Vi gently lowered Rose onto the back seat. No one waved them off. Billy Bob stood in front of the car's bonnet in a top hat and tails, with the air of an undertaker leading a funeral procession. For once, he had nothing to say. On Mrs Sproat's insistence, they had said goodbye to Lady Symes earlier that morning.

'Tell her you're off to boarding school,' said the housekeeper.

'You look fat,' was all Lady Symes had said as Rose approached her on the chaise longue. Then added, 'Tell Mrs Sproat she is feeding you too much. Boarding school? Yes, that will help. Now I must rest. What are you wearing?'

'Let's go,' said Vi, taking Rose's arm. 'I think you look magnificent.'

Mrs Sproat had found her old wedding suit and altered it to fit Rose.

'I'll not be wearing it again. Don't know why I have kept it all these years.'

The description Mrs S had given of Miss Primrose's nursing home as a place for the rest, recuperation and hidden misfortunes of gentlewomen may have been accurate once, but it was obvious to Vi as they drove towards it down a rutted track that the war had given it a new role. Two army ambulances were parked outside the front door. Soldiers were gathered in small groups on the lawn alongside the drive.

'Soldiers!' exclaimed Vi. 'But not normal soldiers?'

'Americans.' It was the only word the chauffeur had uttered.

Rose had been dozing for most of the journey, but her head shot up, a look of terror on her face. 'Why are they here?' she whispered.

They were directed to the back of the main house to an ugly single-storey concrete building with a corrugated iron roof. A starched nurse in an elaborate white hat came to meet them.

'You call me Matron,' she said as Vi got out of the car. 'I don't want any trouble from either of you. She's caused enough already. Worst child I've ever had to look after.' Matron glared at Rose on the back seat.

Miss Primrose had gone up in the world. Vi wondered how much Sir Reginald must be paying her to take them in.

'This is a hospital for very sick men. Men who risk their lives for us all ...'

A small army jeep drove past. It had no roof. The driver waved at Vi and tooted his horn. 'How ya doing?' he shouted. Vi waved back; his cheeriness was infectious.

'... enough of that. You're not to mix with any of the men. Here's your room.' Matron jabbed a finger at Vi. 'You will collect food from the kitchens for you both. And as for you, you're a disgrace.' Rose was trying to climb out of the back seat. Her shape made it difficult. Vi gave her a helping hand then turned to face Matron.

'Don't you dare speak to her like that! You will call her Miss Rose and treat her with respect, or I'll make sure you never get a penny from her father. He is expecting me to report back on everything that happens here and the care given to his beloved daughter.' The lie slipped out so easily Vi thought it sounded convincing.

'Beloved! Hmm! I've got better things to do,' said Matron, turning back towards the house.

It was impossible to avoid seeing the men. They were everywhere and they were delighted to see the two girls. 'Hey! How ya doing?' was the usual greeting as Vi made her way to the kitchen every morning. 'Let me carry that for you, ma'am,' as she took the basket of food back to Rose. Despite their bandages and crutches, the soldiers had a relentless cheerfulness that Vi loved. Billy Bob took to riding the jeeps that busied around the hospital grounds, singing and saluting as he went.

'Howdy, Miss Vi. I come from Alabama with my banjo on my knee.'

One of the soldiers had a harmonica and would sit on the step outside Vi and Rose's block playing lively tunes that Vi would tap out with her foot.

'I've gotta baby girl back home. She came just before I got on the ship, so I ain't hardly met her yet,' he told her. One of his eyes was heavily bandaged. 'I only need the one eye to see her when I get back and I've still got the one. One-eyed Wayne has a mighty fine ring to it, don't ya think?'

It was impossible to coax Rose outside. She sat staring into space. Vi never asked her about America. That something terrible had happened was obvious. Vi wanted to absorb all Wayne's optimism and give it to Rose, but all she could do was hold the other girl's hand and be there night and day until the baby came.

CHAPTER 14

Violet – Rose's Missing Chapter

*T*hen began another chapter of Rose's life. She never talked about it.

'I think the baby's coming,' was enough to send Vi dashing across to the main house in the dark of one night. The kitchen door was locked. Vi raced to the front of the house, where light spilled out from the main hallway. A nurse was on duty behind a desk.

'You've got to come. Miss Rose is having the baby. Tell Matron.'

They took Rose away. Vi was holding her when they came. Rose was bent over, moaning in pain.

'Don't leave me, Vi. Don't let them take me.'

Gentle hands took Vi's and a gentle voice said, 'Let her go. We know what we're doing, you're better off here. There is no place for you. We've got you, Rose. It's going to be okay.' Rose went limp and leant heavily against the two nurses as they led her from the room. And that was it. Vi lay down on the bed and waited for another day to start.

There was no word of Rose for two days. It was only Wayne that made the time bearable for Vi.

'It's okay, kiddo. Babies come when they come and they come all the time. You just have to wait. My May took all night and all day to come into the world, and when she came she was as perfect as a dewdrop at dawn. How about a game of cards?' Billy Bob always sat with them for cards; propped up against a tree, a large cigar hanging out of his mouth, a tumbler of whisky in one hand and a fan of playing cards in the other.

Rose reappeared as suddenly as she had left. Wheeled back across the grass in a wheelchair. Sitting as still as a marble statue.

'Where's the baby?

Where's the baby?' Vi said it louder the second time. Rose didn't move. The nurse stopped pushing the wheelchair and held up her hand as if to silence Vi.

'What have you done with the baby?' Vi was shouting now.

'He's gone,' said Rose quietly. 'I don't want him.'

'That's not the plan. That's not the plan, Rose.' Vi gripped the arms of the wheelchair. She wanted Rose to feel her panic, her anger.

'I'm tired, Vi. Just let him go. The plan was never really a plan, was it? Just a story we told ourselves.'

The nurse helped Rose into the bed. 'She needs rest. The best thing you can do is calm down. Matron says you are both being collected in the morning. It's better this way. She's young, she'll get over all this, and so will you. The baby will go to a fine family. It's better for everyone.'

The nurse's harsh words came to Vi from a distance. Her brain was racing ahead. She needed to find Wayne.

He was not far away, in one of the outbuildings that served as a workshop where the injured men could keep their hands busy. Wayne was whittling wooden farm animals for May.

'Hey, Vi, whaddaya think of this little fella?' Wayne held up a lump of wood vaguely resembling a cow. 'Any news?'

'Yes, but they've taken it. It's going to be my baby, mine and George's. It's all planned and now ... and now...'

'Whoah! Slow down there. What's this plan?'

So Vi told him. 'But they're not sticking with it. They are going to give the baby away. I need a jeep, Wayne. You've got to help me.' Wayne listened as Vi spilled out all that she knew and all that she had planned. He let out a low whistle as she finished.

'That's quite a plan. They're sending me back to France, not home. I heard this morning. It seems a sore head and a dodgy eye won't prevent me lifting and carrying in the field hospital. I may never get to meet my May, Vi. Okay. I'll get you your jeep, but you're gonna need diapers and milk, bottles and a way to smuggle him out.'

Vi had not thought of any of that. All she knew was she had to find the baby and take him away before anyone else did.

'Give me an hour. I'll try and sort everything. Meet me by the main gate in an hour. Everybody will be having lunch then. You'll need a map. The village is Chalworth. I think it took about an hour to get here. I can find the farm once we get to Chalworth. Thank you, Wayne.'

Vi ran back to the little concrete house. There was no sign of Billy Bob. Rose was asleep when she got there. The air-raid drill was pinned to the back of the door. Rose ripped it off and wrote a short note for Rose on the back:

I'm sticking with the plan, Rose. It's a good plan and I can make it work. We can both start again, Rose. When you get back, make them send you to St Martha's. You'll be fine there. Tell Pamela I sent you. It's over and it's beginning. Vi

She left the note alongside Rose's bed. 'Now let's go find a baby.'

Nobody took any notice of Vi. 'Just getting milk for Miss Rose,' she said, taking one of the jugs off the dresser and slipping a large wicker basket over her arm into which she dropped a pile of starched napkins. The back stairs led up to the attic rooms where the nurses slept. He would be up there. 'Please let him be up there.' Vi had not given any thought to prayers for some time, but long forgotten words came back to her.

O Lamb of God, that takest away the sins of the world, hear our prayer.

Vi paused at the top of the stairs. Muffled but unmistakable, she heard the soft cry of a baby. She followed the plaintive wail and there he was, lying swaddled in a makeshift cot. A drawer on top of a trestle table, an empty bottle alongside. His face was red and puckered. His dark hair seemed wet against his tiny head.

'Oh!' Vi felt air expelling from her lungs. She had a sense of falling from a great height and landing on a surface so soft and sweet that her whole body seemed to melt into it. She picked up the tiny bundle and held it against her. The crying stopped. Time stopped. 'I've got you,' she whispered.

It was easy to smuggle the baby out through the main body of the house. Vi walked slowly, with the basket swinging gently at her side. She felt more exposed as she made her way down the main drive with its sweeping lawns on either side, but she might as well have been invisible for all that anyone saw her. Billy Bob was watching her. Vi sensed him but could not see him; footfall on the gravel, a breath of air as something passed her, a slight distortion of the light. The baby let out a small cry. There was Wayne leaping out of the jeep to help her.

'Turn left then keep going. The farm is at the end of the track. That's Rose's house over there.' Vi pointed across the road, shouting to be heard above the engine noise. The baby had slept throughout the drive to Chalworth. His basket was tucked in the footwell of the jeep at Vi's feet. People had stopped and stared as the army jeep careered through the village. Wayne gave them all a cheery, 'Howdy!' Vi let her thoughts drift; her and the baby, George coming out to meet them, little Mousie raising his head when he heard her voice, but the farmyard was empty. It looked unswept; hens pecked about the corners and a half-emptied trailer stood outside the barn. There were signs of activity but no sign of anyone.

'What a place,' said Wayne, leaping down to help Vi and her basket out of the jeep. The baby was stirring. 'He'll be needing some of that milk and a fresh diaper. Let's get him inside.'

Vi led the way to the back door. 'It's always left open. Where is everyone?' An elderly dog appeared in the doorway and gave a solitary bark before settling back on his haunches, duty done.

'Hello, Meg,' said Vi. 'Where's your master?'

Meg cocked her head towards the meat larder that led off the kitchen. Mr Turner appeared in the doorway. He did not seem surprised to see Vi or to hear the cries of a newborn baby. He looked worn and shrunken, as if all the stuffing had been taken out of him.

'He's gone, Vi. Went the day after you left. Just upped and went. Left a note saying he was signing up. Gone to fight for his country. I haven't heard anything since.'

The baby's cry was getting louder. Vi ignored it. 'He's too young. He can't have done. Why is no one sticking with the plan?'

Mr Turner shook his head and turned away, as if to blot out the past and the scene in front of him. 'You best be going too, Vi. You and that baby are not wanted here.'

'No! Wait! We've got nowhere else to go. This is Wayne. He drove me here. None of this is the baby's fault. He needs feeding.'

'I've got this,' said Wayne. He took the crying baby from Vi's basket and held it against him with one hand, while the other poured some of the milk they had brought into the empty bottle and set it inside the large kettle that kept warm on the range. 'Settle yourself here, Vi, and I'll show you what to do.' Wayne pointed to the high-backed chair alongside the range. Mr Turner turned back and watched. Meg circled around the chair and sniffed the tiny bundle as Wayne lowered it onto Vi's lap and handed her the bottle.

'He's a plucky little fella,' said Wayne as the baby started to suck.

'Don't hold it quite so high, Vi.' Mr Turner crossed over to where Vi sat and slowly adjusted the angle of the bottle in her hand. 'It's like the lambs. They can't take it so fast when they are new. He'll soon get the hang of it.'

Vi smiled up at him. 'I'm going to call him William,' she said.

Epilogue – A Year Later

'And the English prize for poetry goes to Rose Symes ...'
The hall erupted with applause and Rose made her way to
the dais to accept a leather-bound copy of the works of Shake-
speare from Miss Stretton.

'Well done,' said Pamela as Rose made her way back to the
seat next to her. 'You jolly well deserve that; your *Autumn
Leaves* poem was brilliant.' The poem was the nearest Rose had
got to talking about her life, but no one knew the truth. She was
not one of the golden leaves tumbling and catching the light;
she was the tree stripped bare, motionless, but still alive in
autumn's soggy gloom, with a rambling rose devoid of all
colour holding fast to the tree's branches.

After her stay in hospital, all Rose held on to – in her hand as
well as her mind – was the note Vi had left her. 'St Martha's,
Pamela' was all Mrs Sproat could get out of her. Rose could not
think about Vi because that would make her think of the baby.
'I need to go to St Martha's,' she told Mrs Sproat. 'Tell them.'

It was Aunt Maud who made it all happen. Mrs Sproat wrote
to her in desperation and she came.

'The school will be a new start for you. I've looked into it
and it seems perfect. Goodness knows what your father was
thinking, sending you off to America. I've spoken to a Miss
Stretton and it's all arranged. Pity that new young maid got
herself in the family way. She must have been a help to you, Mrs
Sproat. Ah well, you won't find girls like that at St Martha's.'

'Come on, the bus is here.' Pamela was calling Rose. The bus
was taking all the girls to the station to get the train home for
the holidays. 'Ma and Pa want to meet you, Rose, and I want to
show you London. Pa says the war is nearly over. We're going to
have such fun.' Pamela wrapped an arm around her friend's

waist. Rose turned for a moment to look at the schoolhouse. It had become her home; it would welcome her back after the holidays. Rose's eye was caught by some movement. In the shadows at the edge of the wood, a young woman was sitting on a pony. Her hair fell loose down her back; her long legs were wrapped around the pony's tummy. The only movement came from the basket strapped across the pony's neck, where two small fists emerged to tangle themselves in the pony's silver-grey mane. The young woman raised her hand in a salute to Rose then slipped back among the trees.

THE END

9 781789 634686